DANNY AND RON ORLIS

AND THE

MEXICAN JUNGLE MYSTERY

DANNY AND RON ORLIS

AND THE

MEXICAN JUNGLE MYSTERY

BERNARD PALMER

Danny and Ron Orlis and the Mexican Jungle Mystery
© 2024 by Bernard Palmer
All rights reserved. First edition 1965.
Second edition 2024.

Scripture quotations from The Authorized (King James) Version. Rights in the Authorized Version in the United Kingdom are vested in the Crown. Reproduced by permission of the Crown's patentee, Cambridge University Press.

Cover image: Adobe Firefly
Character illustrations: John Ball
Editor: Charlene Miskimen

Aneko Press Youth

www.anekopress.com

Aneko Press, Life Sentence Publishing, and our logos are trademarks of Life Sentence Publishing, Inc.
203 E. Birch Street
P.O. Box 652
Abbotsford, WI 54405

JUVENILE FICTION / Religious / Christian / Action & Adventure

Paperback ISBN: 979-8-88936-020-9

eBook ISBN: 979-8-88936-021-6

10 9 8 7 6 5 4 3 2 1

Available where books are sold

CONTENTS

CHAPTER 1

SUMMER PLANS

It was late spring. Ron Orlis and Darlene Snyder had been cramming for finals at Cedarton Bible Institute for the past week. They had been staying up late at night and getting up at five in the morning to get in extra hours of study before the all-important exams. They saw each other only briefly between classes, or occasionally at mealtime.

Ron was standing in the food line one noon when Darlene came up behind him.

"Hello, stranger."

He looked back, his eyes lighting up. "Hi, Darlene," he said. "How're things going these days?"

She groaned. "I don't know whether I'll live through the next week or not. I've never studied so hard in my life."

They got their food and went across the dining hall to a table.

"Have you heard from the mission yet?" Ron asked. "Do you know what part of Canada you'll be working in this summer?"

"I just got a letter today asking if I would be interested in holding vacation Bible schools in Manitoba and Saskatchewan." Darlene took a letter from her purse. "Betty and I will be starting in a little town northeast of Saskatoon and working east."

Ron toyed with his water glass momentarily. "Sounds as though you'll have a full schedule."

"What about you, Ron?" she asked. "Are your plans completed for the summer?"

He nodded. "Everything is working out OK, I guess. I got final word a few days ago that the team with whom I'm going to Mexico will be leaving ten days or so after school is out."

"It sounds as though you've got an exciting summer ahead of you."

"It's going to be a lot of hard work. We'll be doing literature work in southern Mexico."

Darlene tried to hide her concern. "Isn't there quite a bit of opposition to the gospel there?"

"Paganism is still a strong force among the Indians," Ron answered, "and those who've been in the area where we're going say that the enemy has started to do a great deal of work, too. They've been able to stir up the people against the missionaries and Christian nationals in many areas."

Darlene's gaze met his, her eyes becoming dark and serious. "You will be careful, won't you?"

"The Lord will take care of us."

"I know," she said, "but I can't help thinking about you going into a place like that. It–it sounds so dangerous."

He laid a hand on her arm tenderly. "Now, that's no way to talk. Besides, I've laid the matter before the Lord. I know in my heart that I'm going where He wants me to go this summer. And that's really all that matters."

Darlene shook her head. "You don't even sound like the same fellow who used to write Roxie and try to explain why it was all right for you to stay out of Bible school."

A strange fire gleamed in Ron's eyes.

"I'm not the same guy, believe me. And I pray God I will never be that guy again." He breathed deeply. "To think Roxie had to give her life to–to wake me up. I'll never get over that."

"Roxie wasn't taken just to wake you up, Ron," Darlene replied. "I honestly believe that God took her Home to wake us all up. I was as shallow and empty as you or any of the other nominal Christians around school until she died. I saw for the first time in my life that I'd better use what time and ability I have for God, because I might not have much time to do so."

Ron nodded. "God has certainly used her death to bring glory to Himself. Who can question it?"

Darlene spoke softly. "'All things work together

for good to them that love God, to them who are the called according to his purpose.'"

* * *

Ron Orlis managed a quick trip back to the Angle to visit his parents before joining the other guys who were going to Mexico for the summer.

"I sure wish I was going to be able to spend the summer here at home," he said reluctantly.

His dad spoke in reply. "Mother and I would love to have you here for the summer, too. But it's much more important for you to be out in the Lord's work."

"I know that." Ron leaned back in the chair. "But I'd still like to be here when Darlene stops by to visit on her way to Canada."

Carl Orlis's eyes lighted.

"You sound as though she's someone very special."

Ron took his time in answering.

"She is someone very special, Dad," he said. "I'm just beginning to realize how special she is to me."

His mother smiled.

"She's a lovely girl, Ron."

"And what makes her even more lovely is the fact that she loves the Lord so deeply. She's more concerned about living for Christ than she is about anything else in the world."

At the dinner table that evening Carl and Mary Orlis asked Ron about the work he would be doing in Mexico.

"It's not too easy for regular missionaries to work in some places down there, but people who pass out literature haven't had too much trouble," he said. "This group we're going with has been able to get the Word of God into the hands of a lot of people who have never before heard that the Lord Jesus Christ died and rose again to save them from the results of their sins." He leaned forward excitedly. "A lot of these people have just learned to read. They're so eager for reading material they'll take almost anything and read it until it falls apart."

Carl Orlis nodded. "Literature is a splendid way of reaching the lost for Christ."

"And, Dad, we've got a Bible correspondence course in Spanish for just a few centavos – just enough to make them value it. It spells out the plan of salvation in terms so plain that no one could misunderstand. They've had many, many conversions through those courses alone."

Mary Orlis voiced a question that had been on their minds since Ron came home and told them he was going to Mexico that summer.

"Tell me, Ron, do you feel as though God wants you in Canada, or do you think He might be leading you to some other field?"

"My heart's in Canada with the Indians, Mom," he said. "The Lord made that so clear to me there's never been any question about it. I'm convinced that is His will for my life. But I feel called to Mexico, too. I don't know just why. It may be because it will give me a chance to serve in a special way as a student. Or it may be because it's an opportunity for me to learn methods that will be a help to me when I do go to Canada."

His mother nodded her agreement.

"I'm so glad of that, Ron. Not that you're going to be in Canada, necessarily, but that you are so sure you are in the center of the Lord's will. That is the only way for a Christian to be truly happy."

"I've found that out by experience, believe me."

There was a momentary silence.

"There's something else I've been wondering about, Ron," his dad put in. "If you spend the summer in Mexico working without salary, what will you do for money next semester? Have you thought about that?"

Ron nodded. "I've done more praying about it than I have thinking about it, Dad. I came to the conclusion that if God wanted me to go to Mexico, He would provide the money for me to go to school. I'm not concerned in the least about it."

Ron Orlis spent a week fishing, resting, and visiting with his parents before leaving for Minneapolis where he was to meet his companions.

When he left, his mother tried to keep him from seeing that she cried a little. But he spotted the tears and chided her gently.

"Now, Mom, you promised."

She smiled. "What's the use of being a mother," she asked, "if you can't act like one once in a while?"

CHAPTER 2

OFF FOR MEXICO

Ron Orlis met the other guys who made up the rest of his party at Minneapolis, and they started for Mexico in the overloaded car. His partner for the summer, a lanky, blue-eyed lad a couple years younger than himself, was from Montana. Glen Talbert had a heavy shock of blond hair, a smile as big as his hat, and the open friendliness of a Westerner. As Ron approached the guys in the hotel lobby, Glen came forward and thrust out his hand.

"My name's Talbert – Glen Talbert. I take it that you're Ron Orlis."

"That's right," Ron said. There was something refreshing and genuine about the towering Westerner. Instinctively Ron liked him.

"From what I hear it looks as though you and I'll be working together."

Ron surveyed Glen approvingly.

"That suits me fine."

The driver, Steve Merrick, who had been standing nearby, noted the time. "Well, if we're going to get down to Mexico, we'd better get with it. We've got a lot of miles to drive."

"OK, Steve." Talbert picked up his battered suitcase and headed for the car. Several steps away he stopped and stared. "What have you got in that galloping jalopy anyway?"

Steve laughed. "A few thousand tracts, a dozen boxes of books, and some assorted bundles of literature we'll be distributing. That's all."

Glen shook his head. "If she was a horse, she'd be bowlegged from trying to carry a load like that."

Ron laughed. "And we've still got our own gear and ourselves to pile in."

"If we were out in Montana," Glen continued, "they'd never let us ride. They'd make us walk and lead her."

"This isn't anything," Steve said. "You should've seen the way we were loaded when we went down to Mexico at Christmastime."

Glen and Ron threw their suitcases into the rack on top of the car and got in beside Steve.

They left Minneapolis and drove south on Highway 65, changing drivers every two hours. The boys drove straight through the first night but stopped at a motel the second. It was midafternoon of the third day when they crossed the border into Mexico.

Steve Merrick drove slowly through the little border town and up into the hills.

"Well," he said quietly, "this is Mexico."

Glen Talbert's gaze drifted across the bleak, treeless hills. "You know," he said, "it doesn't look a bit different than it does in Texas."

"It is different," Steve continued, "believe me."

Ron Orlis nodded. "Just wait until we get into one of these little towns and try to buy something to eat or ask directions. You'll soon find out that it's different."

The former Montana cowhand grinned. "No sweat at all. I will speak to them in my flawless Spanish."

Ron Orlis snorted. "Flawless Spanish? If that's Spanish you've been trying on us, I've got another name for it."

"It should be flawless Spanish." Glen's eyes were merry. "We had a Mexican family work for us awhile three or four years ago. I picked up a lot of Spanish from them." He paused. "Of course, there may have been some Indian dialect thrown in."

"I guess I shouldn't be saying anything," Ron went on. "I don't imagine my Spanish is so hot either. I'm just praying I know enough to be able to get along."

They drove through another village. The smile left the Montana lad's face.

"Just look at those poor people. And to think they've never had a chance to hear the good news that the Lord Jesus died on the cross and rose again to save them from sin." A faraway look came into his eyes. "It makes a fellow want to stop right here and go to work."

Steve Merrick nodded gravely. "I know just how you feel. But we've prayed this through and honestly believe it's best for you and Ron to go down to southern Mexico." A wistful sigh escaped his lips. "Perhaps the time will come when we get enough funds and students to hit all of these areas. Nothing would make us happier. But right now we have to go where it seems the need is the greatest."

"I'm sure you're right. But I don't see how it could be any greater than it is right here," Glen said.

The following evening they drove into Mexico City and located the house of Ramon de La Sylva, a Christian national who had invited them to stay with him. His wife, Maria, came to the door – a robust, smiling woman who spoke English haltingly.

"Ramon, he not home," she said. "You come in, yes?" They followed her into the modest little home. "Ramon at park." She picked up a tract from the table and extended it toward each of the boys in a sudden gesture.

Steve nodded and glanced at his companions. "I think he must be passing out tracts."

He asked Maria about it in halting Spanish.

"Sí!" Her round face beamed at being understood and she made the motions again. "Sí. Many papers he take. Come back – all gone. Somebody Christian he become, maybe."

It was dark when the slight, thin-faced Mexican returned to his home, his tracts distributed. He spoke a little better English than his wife. After welcoming the boys profusely, he sat down next to Ron.

"You bring more tracts, no?"

Ron explained that they had brought tracts for him.

Ramon nodded his pleasure. "It is good. Very good. Today I could give away twice as many as I have. And the Bibles, they are gone."

"We've got Spanish Bibles along, too," Ron told him, "and some other books to sell. And by the time we get those distributed, the boxes of literature we shipped by express should be here. Oh, we've got plenty of literature, all right."

While Ron and Steve talked with the dedicated young Christian lay worker, Glen went out to the car, got a sample of their literature, and brought it in to show him.

"Sí." He smiled his delight. "Sí. Many souls will be saved with these."

"That is what we've been praying for ever since we knew we would be coming on this trip, Señor de La Sylva," Ron said.

Ramon nodded. "Sí. It is what we all wait and pray for. But there are so many here in Mexico who have not taken Christ as their Savior." His eyes darkened. "So many do not know the Lord Jesus died for their sin."

Steve would have asked a question at that moment, but Ramon's wife came into the room just then and called them to dinner. When they finished eating, the boys from America began to question the youthful national about his ministry and the need for a gospel witness in his country. Ron did most of the talking.

"Do you and your wife have a church to go to?"

"Sí." He nodded vigorously. "Sí, Maria and I, we have church to go to. It is small, but we go every Sunday."

"Somehow I had the idea you wouldn't be able to find a church that preached the gospel within walking distance."

Steve turned to Ron. "You may not know it," he said, "but Ramon is the fellow who won so many to Christ last year. He's the one the guys were all talking about."

"No," the Mexican replied quickly. "I talk – like the Bible say. I water. God makes the flower to bloom. Give Him the glory."

Ron persisted in questioning. "How many fellows did you pray with last year, Ramon? Do you remember?"

He shook his head. "Twenty-eight, maybe – or thirty. I forget."

Ron's eyes widened. Glen Talbert leaned forward and broke in incredulously.

"Do you mean to tell us that you prayed with twenty-eight or thirty people in just one year?"

"No," he answered simply. "Since May 1. A month and a week maybe."

* * *

They were all exhausted from the long, tiring ride, but Ron wasn't able to sleep. Every time he closed his eyes he could see the streets of Mexico City, a surging mass of people – people who had never heard that they were headed for an eternity apart from Christ.

It was small wonder that Ramon worked so desperately passing out tracts, selling Bibles, and talking with as many as he could about the Lord Jesus Christ.

A prayer welled up in his heart. Oh, that he might have the same burden for the lost that this Mexican national had!

The following morning when they got up, Ramon was already sitting at the table, bent over a map of the city. When they finished breakfast, he showed them the map and the areas he had marked with a pencil.

"I take you out to this place." He pointed to a spot on the map. "You and this man with the big hat go here. I take you as soon as you are ready."

Ron and Glen were the first ones to be let out to work. They got out of the car and loaded their arms with literature.

Steve noted the time. "We'll be back for you in about an hour."

The two of them started up the street, handing out tracts to those they met and trying to ignore the icy, unfriendly stares that came their way.

Midway in the second block a burly individual bumped into Ron deliberately, knocking the tracts from his arms. His eyes glared belligerently into those of the young American.

"Watch where you go!" Anger tinged his voice.

"I–I'm sorry," Ron said. "I didn't mean to bump you.

The stranger swore in Spanish and two or three others as dark and hostile as he swaggered out of the shadows to glare at him.

"You make trouble?" another stranger demanded, jostling Ron arrogantly.

In desperation Ron looked about, but Glen was not in sight. Ron was alone! Alone and cornered by three ill-tempered troublemakers!

CHAPTER 3

PEDRO

The men crowded closer to Ron, anger and arrogance twisting their dark faces. For a brief moment the speaker glared at him belligerently. But Ron stood his ground.

"What you got there?" He snatched for a tract in Ron's hand.

The young man smiled. "They're free," he answered. "You can have copies for your friends, too, if you'd like."

One of the men read the title aloud in Spanish.

"'God is the Answer.' Religion? Bah!"

Ron shook his head. "We didn't come here to tell you about religion." The sweat came out on his face as he struggled to find the words in Spanish to say what he meant. "We came to introduce you to the Lord Jesus Christ."

Two or three people stopped and were watching

curiously. The biggest of the three men frowned and swore at them.

"Come!" He grasped Ron Orlis by the arm and twisted it savagely. "We talk to you!" Ron jerked away.

"If you want to talk to me, you'll have to talk right here," he said calmly. "I'm not going anywhere else to talk."

The stranger swore again in Spanish and spoke hurriedly to his companions. One of them grasped Ron by the other arm.

"You do as Manuel say and you not get hurt!"

They started to force Ron into a nearby alley that was already dark with shadows. He braced his feet and jerked free. In the same motion, he swung his book-loaded briefcase with all his strength. It thudded into the big man's stomach.

"Ugh!" A grunt exploded from the man called Manuel. Involuntarily he grasped his stomach with both hands.

At that instant a passerby saw what was happening.

"Police! Police!" The shrill cry echoed along the street.

Even as he shouted, he ran to Ron's assistance, and it seemed that everyone on the street joined him. Manuel and his pals saw them coming and fled. Half a minute later, the police charged past Ron in a desperate but futile effort to catch them.

For a brief space of time all was confusion. Once things began to quiet down a bit, the man who had first sounded the alarm turned to Ron Orlis.

"Are you all right?"

The youthful American thrust out his hand gravely. He knew that his face was still ashen and fear tingled up his spine. "And I have you to thank for that, señor."

Concern still marked the well-dressed Mexican's face.

"Those men are not Mexicans." He spoke in very acceptable English. "You would not think that all Mexicans are like them?"

Ron smiled. "Of course not."

Impulsively he took an inexpensive Bible from his briefcase, wrote his name and address in it, and gave it to his rescuer.

"Gracias!" The man's face beamed. "Gracias, señor."

At first Ron did not notice that there was a boy standing nearby. He did not notice him until the others left and the two of them were alone. A timid smile crept speculatively to the boy's lips.

"I am glad you not hurt, Señor Yanqui. Those bad men."

Something about the boy was appealing. He was only a lad, Ron saw at a glance – a thin, hungry-looking lad in ragged clothes and shoes so worn that they scarcely clung to his feet. His hair was straight and long and his face a swarthy brown. His features were somewhat different from most of those about him.

Probably an Indian lad, Ron reasoned, who had come into Mexico City from the hills to try and find work.

"How old are you?"

The boy's smile grew bolder.

"Fourteen."

"You speak English well for fourteen."

"Not so well as I like to speak. I guide Americanos in summer."

Ron saw that the boy's gaze was fixed on the briefcase in his hand.

"Very nice, isn't it?" He held it up so the boy could see the beautiful leather carving. "I bought it here in Mexico City."

The boy shook his head. "It is not the case I look at." He hesitated. "I think about the book you give to man. It was Bible, no?"

"Yes, it was a Bible."

A wistful longing came into the boy's eyes.

"I have always want Bible."

"Would you like to buy one? I have a nice Bible for sale – cheap."

Sorrowfully the boy shook his head.

"No pesos. I guide many Americanos and get pesos to buy Bible maybe."

Ron Orlis rubbed a finger along the side of his nose thoughtfully. There was something about this lad – something that set him apart from the others on the street.

"What is your name?"

"Pedro," he said simply.

There was a moment's silence.

"Do you know the Lord Jesus Christ as your Savior, Pedro? Are you a Christian?"

The flames kindled in the boy's dark eyes.

"Sí!" The smile spread across his broad face. "And you, Señor Yanqui. You love Jesus Christ?"

"That is why I am here – to help tell your people about the Lord Jesus Christ."

The boy's face grew serious.

"A man come to our village to tell about Jesus, but I only one who – how you say – become Christian."

"And you haven't had a Bible?"

"No, señor," Pedro replied. "But I get one. As soon as I save pesos, I get one."

"Have you been going to church, Pedro?" Ron asked.

"Church?" A blank look came to his face. "What is church?"

That did it.

"We're supposed to sell our Bibles, Pedro, but I'm going to give you one."

The boy stared at him incredulously, as though this couldn't possibly be true.

"You have Bible to give to me?"

"I'm going to give you a Bible. Of course, you'll have to come with me to the place where we're staying. I don't have another inexpensive Bible with me this afternoon. But I have one back at my room."

The boy nodded his head. "A Bible for Pedro? Gracias."

Ron grinned. "I want you to have it," Ron said, "but why don't you call me Ron? That's my name."

"Sí." His expression did not change.

"That's right," Ron repeated. "I want you to call me Ron. My name is Ron Orlis."

"Ron Orlis." He spoke slowly. "Ron Orlis."

"Everybody calls me Ron."

"Ron." His lips formed the words. "Ron . . . Ron Orlis . . . and gracias for the Bible. Gracias."

Pedro went with Ron while he distributed tracts and stopped in a few places to sell books. At the appointed time they went back to the place where they were to meet the others. Glen was already there waiting for them.

"Whatever happened to you, Ron?" he asked. "I thought maybe somebody grabbed you and put you in the pokey."

"We did have a little excitement," Ron replied. "When we get back to the house, I'll tell you all about it."

He introduced Pedro to the others and told them about the Bible he was going to give to the young Indian boy.

As they started home, Steve turned to their new passenger. "Where do you live, Pedro?" he asked.

"Far from here." He motioned toward the south. "Many days' walk."

Immediately Ron was interested. The boy was much younger than Indian boys in Canada when they left home – at least for good.

"How did you come to leave your village?"

The shadow of memory fell across the lad's face.

"When I take Jesus as my Savior, man say I go home and tell father and mother."

Ron nodded. "It's best to do that," he said. "I've seen too many people who have tried to keep their salvation to themselves. It usually doesn't work that way."

"I tell them," Pedro said, "but they not happy. They angry, much angry."

Ron could understand that, too. He had seen the parents of kids in Minnesota and Canada who became furious when their children confessed their sin and accepted Christ as their Savior.

The Indian boy continued slowly, as though even remembering what had happened was painful.

"They took sticks and beat Pedro. At night Pedro run away. No can go back."

Glen broke in. "You mean you don't dare go back to your own village?" he asked.

The boy looked at him blankly but did not say anything more.

When they got out to the house, Ramon and Maria insisted that Pedro stay and eat with them. He thanked them profusely. After supper he moved to a chair near the door, fondling the Bible Ron had brought and given him. Suddenly he turned to Ron.

"Why you have Bibles?" he asked seriously.

"So we can help your people to find Christ as their Savior."

"My people?" The question stood in his eyes. "My people in my village?"

At first Ron did not exactly understand him.

"Yes, Pedro," he said. "We came to help people like those in your own village."

Tears came to the usually stoic Indian lad's eyes.

"Every day I pray that someone go to my village and tell my father and my mother about Jesus." He straightened with new determination. "I go with you!"

Ron stared at him helplessly. How could he explain to this simple Christian boy that he wouldn't be able to go to his particular village? How could he tell him that he wouldn't be able to talk with his parents about Christ? Ron struggled for words.

CHAPTER 4

RON'S DECISION

Ron stared sorrowfully at Pedro.

"You will come to our village?" Pedro's voice was pleading. "You will come and talk to my people about Jesus?"

Ron tried to look into the boy's dark eyes, but he could not.

"I – I'd like to," he stammered. "Honestly, I would. But I can't. The plans have already been made for me to go somewhere else."

Realization came slowly to the youthful Indian. The light died in his eyes and his bony face grew somber.

"But, señor," he protested, "I pray. All these months I pray."

"Maybe we can come another time." Ron spoke lamely. "Next year–"

"Next year?" Dismay flooded over Pedro.

Ron winced. A year could as well be a century to a

boy of fourteen, especially a boy who had been driven from his home and loved ones because he dared to name Jesus as his Savior. "We can talk to the director of our group. Maybe he can send somebody else to the village of your parents later in the summer."

Pedro swallowed hard.

"When I see you are Christian, God seem almost to speak to Pedro," he said, his voice dull with disappointment. "It seem almost like He say, 'I send the señor. He talk to your father. He talk to your mother. He make them to listen!'" The boy leaned forward, eyes pleading desperately. "Would God make mistake, Señor Ron? Would he tell Pedro He send you to village and not do it?"

Ron looked helplessly about the room and back again at Pedro.

"No," he said hesitantly, "God doesn't make mistakes. But–" His voice trailed off. How could he explain it? How could he tell the young Indian that it might well be the longing of his own heart that made him think God was leading the two of them to the little village where he used to live?

Or was it?

There was a long, painful silence.

"Missionary man say if Pedro ask God, He will make Christians of father and mother, even little sisters. Every day, two, maybe three times, Pedro talk to God about it for so long. You think God hear?"

"Of course, God hears."

The youthful Indian sighed wearily.

"You think God care about Pedro?" he persisted. "You think maybe someday God answer Pedro's many prayings?"

It was all Ron could do to speak.

"Pedro," he said, "God cares for you. He cares for your father and mother, too."

The boy took a deep breath.

"Then why He not send someone for to talk to them?"

"God is faithful. He will send someone to talk to them. Someday He will answer your prayers."

Although the boy nodded gravely, his eyes did not reflect any confidence at all. The lights had gone out, leaving them cold and desolate.

Ramon, who had been sitting quietly, broke into the conversation.

"It is getting late, Pedro," he said. "You stay the night with us?"

The boy stirred.

"No, I go."

"But it is already dark and it is far to where you live. You stay the night?" He smiled warmly.

Maria's smile joined that of her husband.

"Sí, you stay here with us this night." She spoke a flood of Spanish that left Ron bewildered and gasping and completely ignorant of what she had said.

Pedro's dark face lit up briefly.

"Sí. I stay, maybe."

They had a time of Bible reading and prayer before

going to bed. Pedro sat quietly, listening but making no comment. The hurt still gleamed darkly in his eyes. Ron could not forget the keen disappointment that seemed to border on despair.

"I've never seen a boy as concerned about the salvation of his parents as Pedro, have you, Glen?" he asked his roommate when they were alone.

His new friend shook his head.

"Of course, he's the first person I've ever met whose parents have turned so completely on him," Glen said. "He knows what it's like to have parents who are outside the Lord. I suppose that's why he's so eager."

Ron got into his pajamas but did not go to bed immediately. He sat on a rickety straight-backed chair and crossed his legs.

"I don't think I've ever hated to do anything as badly as I hated to tell Pedro that I couldn't go back to his village with him to talk to his parents about Christ."

Glen nodded. "I know. I felt the same way."

"He seemed so sure God had sent us to witness to his parents and was so crushed when he found out it won't be possible for us to go there."

Ron got to his feet and crossed the narrow room.

"I wish I were directing this outfit," he said. "I'd go down there myself, starting the first thing in the morning."

They turned out the lights and went to bed. Ron dropped off to sleep almost immediately but awakened sometime later to toss fitfully for an hour or more. He could still see the look of dismay, the keen disappointment in the Indian boy's eyes. He could still feel the hurt that must have been Pedro's. And the boy had suffered so much – so very much – for his faith.

It wasn't as though Pedro was asking something for himself, Ron reasoned. All he wanted was for someone to go down to the little village where his parents lived and talk to them about the Savior.

And there was no one to go. No one.

When Ron Orlis got up the following morning, he was still greatly disturbed about it. Pedro was smiling as he came out of the bedroom and took a chair near the table.

"Good morning."

"Good morning, Pedro. You look as though you slept well last night."

"Sí."

Ron wanted to talk with the Indian lad alone, to tell him that he was very much concerned about his parents and was going to be much in prayer that God would send someone to the village to witness to them. However, Steve, Glen, and the others came in almost immediately, and there was no opportunity.

At the breakfast table everyone began to talk and it seemed as though Pedro was forgotten. He sat very quietly, staring at his plate and saying little. It was not until the time came for prayer after their Bible reading that he spoke.

"Señor Ron," he said, tensely, "you do something for Pedro, no?"

Ron smiled. "If I can."

"You pray that God speak to the heart of my father and mother when they hear the gospel?"

"Of course I will," Ron said. "And I'll be praying that God will send someone to talk to them."

"He has." The Indian lad spoke simply. "I go."

Ron stared.

"You!"

"Sí!"

"But I thought they beat you when you were there, Pedro," he exclaimed. "I thought they said they'd kill you if you ever came back."

The Indian avoided answering him directly.

"God will take care of me."

Ramon spoke in Spanish. "You cannot go, Pedro," he said. "You told us last night how they beat you and how afraid you are to go back. You cannot do this. It will be too dangerous."

"But I must!" Fear set Pedro's lips to quivering, but determination glinted in his dark eyes. Quickly he got to his feet. "Gracias, señor and señora. You pray for Pedro while he goes, yes?"

With that he turned and fled from the house.

Ron half rose from his chair. "Pedro!" he cried.

Ramon shook his head. "It is no use. He is gone. He not come back."

Ron Orlis settled back in his chair slowly. The color faded from his cheeks and perspiration gleamed on his forehead.

"The poor guy," he muttered. "The poor little guy."

Nobody else said a word.

"If–if only there was some way we could help him."

Steve closed the Bible and pushed it aside.

"I wish we'd known about the village earlier," he said. "There's no reason why we couldn't have included it in our plans."

Ron's eyes brightened. "Don't you think we could do it anyway, Steve?" he asked. "Couldn't we work things out somehow?"

"I'd like to, but it's awfully late. Everything's been arranged."

"But Glen could take care of the work where he and I were going, and I could go down with Pedro."

Ramon broke in suddenly. "Sí. I can find Mexican friend to go with Glen. Already I know of someone."

"That would be great." Ron leaned forward, his excitement growing. "We could cover twice as much territory that way."

Glen nodded. "Sounds like a good idea to me."

Steve was still unconvinced.

"We've always sent teams out by twos," he said.

"I don't like the idea of separating you."

"Look, Steve," Ron persisted. "We're both older than the average guy who comes down on a project like this, and we've both done our share of knocking around. We can take care of ourselves."

At last the director agreed reluctantly. "But it's against my better judgment," he acknowledged.

"Thanks, Steve." Ron jumped to his feet. "Ramon, do you think we can catch Pedro before he leaves Mexico City?"

The national shrugged his shoulders.

"That I not know. He get on bus maybe. Maybe he catch ride."

Ron was halfway to the door.

"Come on, guys," he said. "Let's go out and look for him. We've got to catch him before he gets away."

The four left the house and drove up the street in the direction Ramon thought Pedro would likely go.

Ron's pulses quickened.

What if they didn't find the boy? What if he got back to that village and his people did something terrible to him because he was a Christian? Ron knew it would be his fault.

"Steve," he exclaimed, "what's the matter with this crate? Won't it go any faster?"

CHAPTER 5

PEDRO WINS

Ron sat quietly in the car, staring straight ahead as Steve drove down one narrow, twisting street after another. They didn't even know for sure where Pedro's village was located, except that it was south. They had to find the boy before he left Mexico City. If they didn't, the opportunity to witness to Pedro's people – at least as far as Ron was concerned – would be lost. Besides, there was no knowing what would happen to the Indian lad if he went back to his village alone.

Ron turned to Ramon.

"What could have happened to Pedro?" he asked with concern. "He couldn't just disappear."

The Christian national shrugged. "Who knows where boy goes?"

"That's right, Ron," Steve put in. "He could have gone to any one of a hundred places. It's going to be mighty hard to find him."

"But we've got to!" Ron's voice betrayed his fear. "We've got to find him." He was silent while they drove a distance of three or four blocks. "He hasn't been gone more than half an hour and he was on foot. He couldn't have gotten too far."

Steve's mouth tightened. "If he stayed on foot. We're not sure of that. He might have gone to the bus depot or somewhere to try and catch a ride at least part of the way back to his village."

Ramon straightened suddenly.

"If he have money," he said, "he go to bus depot for sure."

Steve turned at the next comer and drove back to the bus depot. The ticket agent remembered Pedro, all right, but he was not there.

"Sí," he said, "a so-small boy come and ask price for ticket, but he have only a few pesos and it cost so many."

Ron's eyes lighted briefly.

"Then he was here?"

"Sí. He was here. But he gone now."

"Thank you. Thank you."

Ramon was almost at the car when he turned back to the ticket agent.

"You see which way he go?"

The agent shook his head and shrugged his shoulders indifferently. "Who would notice the way an Indian boy goes?"

When they were once more moving down the street in the car Ron turned to his companions.

"Now where do we look?" he asked.

Their Mexican friend considered a moment.

"Pedro say he walk to get here," he recalled. "Maybe he start to walk back."

"That's right, Ramon," Steve said. "We can look on the roads that lead south out of town."

Ron expelled his breath thoughtfully. If only he hadn't been so short with Pedro. If only he had stopped the boy when he went to leave. If only – Questions probed, unanswered, into his tortured mind.

By this time it was almost noon. Life in Mexico City would be grinding to a halt for the traditional midday siesta. Steve drove along the main highway that led south out of town.

"I can't understand it." Ron looked at his watch for the fourth time within the hour. "It hasn't been very long since he left the house. He hasn't had time to get very far is what I'm trying to say. He's just got to be around somewhere."

"That's what I keep telling myself," the director put in. "But we still haven't found him."

"Do you suppose–?" Ron stopped short. "There he is!"

Steve slammed on the brakes and glanced wildly about. "Where is he? Where?"

"In that big high-wheeled cart." There was a brief silence. "See him?"

They drove alongside the cart, honking and waving at Pedro until he climbed off the slow-moving vehicle and came over to them.

"Señor." Concern stood full in his eyes. "There is trouble?"

"Not now." Ron's grin broadened. "Not now. Everything's fine."

Questions gleamed in Pedro's eyes.

"What you mean?" he demanded. "What happen?"

"Nothing yet. We just came to tell you that I am going to be able to go down to your village with you after all."

It took a moment or two for his words to register in the young Indian's mind. When it did his entire being seemed to glow.

"Señor. Señor Ron." He repeated the salutation several times.

Finally Ron broke in.

"I feel the same way about it that you do, Pedro," he said. "But of course the fact that I'm able to go down there doesn't necessarily mean that your family is going to be saved. God may work that way, and He may not."

"Sí. Sí. Pedro know," the boy answered. "But God answer prayer." His smile grew even broader and more radiant, if possible. "I pray. Oh, how I pray, and God say to me, 'Pedro, I hear you. I think maybe I send that Señor with you to village.' Even when I am on cart alone I think, *Señor Ron, he is one to help Pedro's father and mother.*" His voice crescendoed. "I not know how you find Pedro and get to village, but I know!"

"You have me as excited about getting to your village as you are," Ron told him.

Back at Ramon's home, Steve got the names of the missionary couple who were working near the Indian lad's village.

"It is Señor and Señora Aldrich." Pedro's smile came again. "They are the ones who tell Pedro of Jesus."

Ron nodded. "Oh, sure. I remember their names now. You told me about them when we first met."

Steve picked up his hat and started for the door. "I've got a friend uptown who has a two-way radio. I'm going up to ask him to get in touch with Rev. Aldrich. I'll be back as soon as I can."

It was almost dusk when Steve returned to the house, but there was no need to ask about the outcome. The answer was written in the smile on his face.

"Everything's set, Ron. When I got talking to Gary Aldrich, I realized we'd met when we went to Bible school together. Used to live in the same dorm."

"I'll bet you'd like to go down there in my place."

"That's what I told him," Steve went on. "Maybe I'll be able to get down there sometime. Right now it's much more important for you and Pedro to get there."

When they were alone, Ron questioned the group leader more pointedly about the area.

"Did Aldrich say anything about the people we'll be working with?" he asked. "Did he tell you what to expect?"

Steve shook his head.

"He didn't have too much to say about them except that the work in that part of Mexico is hard – very hard."

"I could tell that by talking with Pedro." Ron leaned back in his chair and crossed his legs thoughtfully. "You'll be praying for us, won't you, Steve?"

"You can be sure of that."

Early the following morning, two hours before the sun was up, Ron and Pedro crawled out of bed and awakened Steve to take them to the bus depot. By sunrise they were jouncing over the highway in a crowded bus.

Pedro was still smiling and shaking his head. "It is wonderful you go with Pedro, Señor," he said for the umpteenth time. "Now, my family, they get chance to hear about Jesus."

"Give the Lord the glory, Pedro," Ron said. "He's the One who worked it out."

The bus ride was long and hot. Both Pedro and Ron were very tired when they finally reached the Yucatan community that was nearest to the area where Gary Aldrich and his wife were working, and where they were to pick them up. Ron and Pedro got off the bus and looked around the dusty, sleepy little town.

"You don't suppose they forgot to come after us, do you?" Ron asked when he saw no one there to meet them.

"They be here." Pedro spoke with great confidence. "They be here."

Even as he spoke a cantankerous old jeep came jouncing around the corner.

"Señor Aldrich!" Pedro cried.

A moment later the ancient vehicle groaned to a stop nearby. Ron went over and introduced himself.

Aldrich turned to his family. "This is my wife, Della," he said, "and my son, Matt."

A gangling lad about Pedro's age, but several inches taller, disengaged himself from the jeep and came over to shake hands.

"Boy, am I glad you're back, Pedro," Matt said. "It's sure been dull around here since you left."

While the two boys talked in Spanish, Gary Aldrich motioned Ron to one side.

"Ever since I told Steve Merrick it was all right for you to come down here, I've been wondering if I did the right thing," he said.

"What do you mean?"

"The witch doctor was furious when Pedro was saved. I had to send the boy away. I was afraid he might be killed."

Ron Orlis nodded. "Pedro told me that, but I thought perhaps he was frightened and exaggerated a little."

"He didn't exaggerate," the veteran missionary said. "I can vouch for that."

Ron's face blanched.

"Do you think he's still in danger?" he asked guardedly.

"I'm sure he is."

Ron rubbed the sweat from his forehead with the back of his bronzed hand. It was a moment or two before he spoke.

"Has anything new happened since Pedro left that would make conditions worse than they were?" he asked.

Gary Aldrich frowned. "I wouldn't say conditions are any worse now than they were when he left," he said, "but they were plenty bad then. So bad I was afraid something terrible might happen to the boy if he stayed."

"Perhaps the witch doctor has forgotten about him by this time."

"You don't know these witch doctors, and especially the witch doctor in Pedro's village. The Indians are all afraid of him."

Ron kicked a pebble with the toe of his boot.

"My brother Danny told me about the witch doctors in Guatemala when he and Kay were on the mission field there," he said. "They were plenty bad."

"They're all alike." Gary Aldrich's voice tightened. "They'll remember a man who crossed them or a boy who took Christ as his Savior if they live for a hundred years. They're a curse to this whole territory."

* * *

Ron wanted to find a place to live right away so he and Pedro wouldn't be imposing on the Aldrich family, but the missionaries wouldn't listen to him.

"We won't hear of your moving right away, Ron," Mrs. Aldrich said firmly. "Do you know how long it has been since Gary and Matt and I have had company we could speak English to? It's been almost a year. You might not want to stay around us, but we're going to keep you just as long as we can."

Gary Aldrich laughed good-naturedly.

"You'd just as well quit protesting, Ron. Della has decided you and Pedro are going to live with us for a while, so that's what you'll be doing. You can't get out of it."

Gary Aldrich had to go for supplies, and it was almost two hours later when they left town to drive to the place where they had built their station.

"I wish it wasn't dark, Ron," Mr. Aldrich said. "I'd like to have you see this country. It's the most beautiful spot I've ever been in."

Ron smiled inwardly. How many times had he heard missionaries make that very same statement when talking about the country where they were serving? Usually they didn't really mean that the country was so beautiful. They meant that their love for the people and the country had made it become beautiful to them.

It was late at night when they got to the mission station. Della Aldrich insisted on fixing a snack of fruit juice and sandwiches.

"I don't feel like going to bed yet," she said. "I just want to talk about home, Ron. How is it back in the States?"

He looked at her blankly. "What do you mean?" She came over and sat across from him. "Just tell us about everything," she said. "I'm starved to hear from home."

They sat in the kitchen for an hour or more. Ron talked about Bible school, about the kids who were in his class, and about Darlene.

Della's face shone.

"I knew there was a 'Darlene' somewhere," she said. "There would have to be."

"That sure isn't the way I planned it," Ron went on. "I can tell you that. I was going to wait until I'd spent a term on the field before I even thought about girls."

"It's better this way." Della spoke with conviction. "You would be so lonely if you were to go out alone. So very lonely."

Her husband broke in good-naturedly.

"Isn't that just like a woman? She hasn't known you more than a few hours and already she's trying to marry you off."

They didn't even know the boys were listening until Matt broke in. "You'd just as well give up, Ron. When Mom starts to work on a marrying project, the guy just doesn't have a chance."

They continued visiting until finally Gary Aldrich got to his feet. "Our days start pretty early around here, Ron," he said. "If we want to get to sleep at all, we'd better turn in."

CHAPTER 6

THE INDIAN VILLAGE

Pedro wanted to go back to his village the very next morning and talk with his parents about the Lord Jesus, but the veteran missionary advised him to wait for a few days.

"There's going to be plenty of time for that, Pedro," he said. "I think we'd better wait and see exactly what the situation is before we barge in over there. We ought to know what the people think about your coming back and having Ron along."

The boy was impatient.

"But, señor," he said, "we know the witch doctor, he want to cause trouble. We know the people are lost without Jesus." His earnest black eyes met Ron's. "What if somebody, he die before he hear about Jesus?"

That was an argument Ron could not answer.

"I think we ought to do as Mr. Aldrich says, Pedro," he countered. "Why don't we pray about it? If the

Lord wants us to go over there, He'll show us that He does." "He wants us to go," the Indian lad said quietly. "That why he bring you down here, señor."

They had a long season of prayer together, the Aldrich family, Ron, and Pedro. When they got to their feet, the Indian boy's face was radiant.

"Matt and I, we pray that God make my family to listen when you tell them of Jesus, señor. A long time we pray."

Ron did not want to go with Pedro to the Indian village. He knew that even before they left Mexico City. But there was a strange driving force that seemed to push them irresistibly onward.

When the boys had gone outside, Ron turned to the missionary.

"What do you think about going over there, Gary?" he asked.

Aldrich shook his head. "Humanly speaking, I hate to see you take Pedro over there," he said. "It's not safe for the boy."

Della Aldrich spoke up. "It isn't any safer for Ron, is it?"

"A little. He hasn't defied the old witch doctor the way Pedro and I have. We are the ones he'll really be after." He laughed dryly, "but it's not going to be any pleasure jaunt for you, Ron. Don't get that in your head."

Ron caught the use of the pronoun *we* immediately.

"We appreciate your willingness to help, Gary," he answered, "but we don't plan on getting you mixed up in this thing. The problem belongs to Pedro and me. We're going to take care of it."

"Now wait a minute. It isn't a matter of your getting us mixed up in anything, Ron," he said. "Our hearts are with these people. We've been praying for Pedro's village ever since we came down here. He's the first convert. He could be the means of opening up the entire village to the gospel. We want to have a part in helping any way we can."

"I guess you're right. I just didn't want you to get mixed up in anything that might hurt your work later. To tell you the truth, I'm not even sure this is the right way to handle the situation."

The missionary thought for a moment.

"Well, Ron," he said after a time, "I can certainly understand how Pedro feels. He wants more than anything else in the world to see his family come to know Christ."

That afternoon Pedro and the missionary's son went off somewhere together and Gary took Ron to the archaeological ruins nearby.

"I'm amazed," Ron exclaimed. "I had no idea the people who used to live here had a culture anything equal to this."

"I've been poking around among these ruins for about ten years and I'm more fascinated by them now than ever," the missionary replied.

Ron walked slowly over to a great sculptured head and stood in awe, admiring the skill and ingenuity of the men who had carved it.

"To think this was carved by people who lived more than one thousand years ago," he said, lowering his voice. "You know, Gary, in some ways their culture was as advanced as ours is today."

"They had amazing skills, that's true. But don't forget, these people made human sacrifices regularly. That was part of their culture, too."

Ron's face grew more serious.

"And most of the people living in this area today are in the same spiritual condition they were in then. They're lost and headed for a Christless eternity in Hell unless someone is able to reach them with the gospel."

"Makes us see the real importance of the work God had called us to do, doesn't it?" Aldrich asked.

The next day the missionary talked with a number of Indian friends about Pedro.

"None of them were from his village," he explained, "but they said they knew his parents and other people who live in his village. None of them had heard anything regarding him."

"What does that mean?" Ron wanted to know.

Aldrich shook his head. "I'm not sure. It may be that the opposition that made it necessary for me to send him away is about gone."

"Do you think we would dare to go into the village?"

The missionary's mouth firmed. "I really think you'd be safe enough – at least on the first trip."

That night they had a long session of prayer. And early the following morning Ron and Pedro went to the village where the Indian boy had lived with his parents. Gary Aldrich planned to make the trip with them, but an emergency came up at the last minute that made it impossible for him to go.

"I think I could go with you tomorrow, Ron," the missionary said.

"Yes," Ron answered, "but Pedro is so excited about going and would be so disappointed if we delay anymore."

"Well, we'll be praying for you."

Ron and Pedro made their way across the hills in the direction of the village. At first Pedro talked quietly, but as time passed and they neared the village, the color went out of his cheeks and sweat moistened his dark forehead.

"Are we getting close?" Ron asked.

"Sí." He stopped and half turned to face the youthful missionary. For the first time Ron saw that fear, stark and ugly, gleamed in the boy's eyes. "Sí, señor. We close."

They stopped on the path and bowed their heads in prayer.

That seemed to buoy Pedro's spirits somewhat. The spring came back in his walk and he smiled again.

"God, He take care of us, won't He, señor?" he asked uneasily.

"Yes," Ron replied, "God will take care of us." Half a mile or so from the village they heard a slight noise on the path ahead of them. A moment later a girl of eight or nine came running toward them.

Pedro stared.

"Rosa!" he gasped.

She stopped dead still. Fear widened her dark eyes and her lower jaw sagged.

"Rosa!"

"Pedro!"

The terror in her angular young face was very evident. She started to speak, but choked. Whirling, she dashed out of sight up the path.

"My sister!" Pedro's voice broke. "My own sister, she run from me!" His eyes were sad and luminous with tears.

Ron paused on the trail.

"I wouldn't blame her for what happened just now if I were you, Pedro," he said. "She wanted to come and talk to you, but she was afraid to."

The boy's lips quivered uncertainly.

"The witch doctor!" His own voice was a hoarse, unnatural whisper.

"That's probably right. I was talking with Gary Aldrich yesterday. He seemed to think that any trouble we might have would be caused by the witch doctor. He said the witch doctor in your village is worse than most."

"Sí, señor," Pedro admitted. "But I think maybe he not so angry with me if his son, Jose, was not my best friend."

"Maybe that's why he's so mad that you became a Christian. He might be afraid that you will get

Jose to become a Christian, too." Ron glanced up the path in the direction of the village. "Don't you think it would be better if we go back to the Aldrich place now and come back here again next week?"

Pedro shook his head firmly.

"No, señor," he said. "We go *now* to tell my mother and father about Jesus."

"All right." In spite of himself, Ron's reluctance showed through. He wanted to go up and talk with the Indians about Christ as badly as Pedro wanted him to, but it would have been hard enough if there had been no opposition. Going this way was just asking for trouble. Yet, he told himself, he had promised Pedro. He had given the Indian lad his word that he would go with him.

They made their way up the steep incline that led to the little Indian village. The settlement looked very much the same as a dozen or more similar villages Ron had seen since arriving in southern Mexico. The little grass-thatched adobe huts were scattered among the trees.

Near the closest house a dark-faced Indian man stripped tough strands from the long, thick leaves of the henequen plant with a steel scraper. His wife, sitting in the doorway, was busy separating the fibers, while their children and a skinny black and white dog played nearby.

Pedro's eyes lighted.

"There's Juan!" He called out the man's name.

Juan looked up. For an instant, recognition glinted on his face. Recognition and friendship. Then they died slowly and he turned away.

"Juan." Pedro's voice caught.

Ron Orlis touched him on the arm.

"He–he is afraid of Pedro, too," the Indian boy said.

Ron smiled a confidence he did not feel.

"I wouldn't worry about that. If he is afraid of you, he'll get over it as soon as he finds out that we're not going to hurt him. Right now, he's probably believing all the lies the witch doctor has told about you. As soon as he finds out those things aren't true, he'll be all right."

"Juan was my very good friend." Doubt and uncertainty showed in Pedro's face. He started forward hesitantly, then stopped and swallowed hard. His hands were trembling slightly and Ron saw that he looked from side to side as though searching for something he did not quite trust or understand – some fearful thing.

"You–you think witch doctor be out, maybe?" His voice was dry and cottony. "You think he catch us?"

"I think we'd have been sure to see him if he'd been around," Ron said. "I don't believe he's going to find us today."

The Indian boy smiled his relief.

Although Ron was glad enough to have the encounter postponed, he knew that the witch doctor would find them. Sooner or later the evil shaman would confront them in the little village or on the path, where there would be no witnesses. Ron shivered uncontrollably although the day was warm.

Neither Ron nor Pedro could help glancing about as they stood talking in the middle of the path. The villagers were eyeing them silently, fearfully. Lips were closed to them. Eyes were dark with hostility and terror.

"Where do your folks live, Pedro?" Ron asked after a time. "We'd better get over and see them."

"This way." He started forward.

In a moment or two, Ron sensed that they were heading toward a hut that was larger than the others. Larger, better thatched, and with two sizable openings for windows. Pedro's parents were not ordinary people in the village, Ron could tell at a glance. They were a family of some position and wealth.

As Ron and the Indian boy drew closer to his home, Pedro's pace slowed and his entire being tensed. His eyes lighted expectantly.

"Do you think they're at home, Pedro?" Ron asked.

"Sí," Pedro said. "My mother, she is home. She never go out except on feast days."

The place looked deserted to the young missionary.

"Maybe she's inside," he said.

Almost as he spoke a slight, dark-eyed figure appeared momentarily in the doorway.

"Lolita!" The name exploded from Pedro's lips.

The child started to run to him.

"Pedro!" she cried happily. "Pedro!"

But a sharp voice sounded from somewhere in the hut.

"Lolita!"

The young girl stopped half a dozen paces from her older brother. Hurt leaped to her eyes. Hurt mingled with fear.

"Pedro." Her voice was a whimper.

"Lolita!" their father ordered from the doorway. "Come here!"

"Father!" Pedro pleaded desperately.

The tall Indian's expression was cold and hostile. "Lolita!" he said again.

The little girl hesitated, but only for an instant. She retreated, step by step. Almost involuntarily, the Indian boy moved toward her and their father.

"Father," he said in desperation in their Indian dialect, "I–I come to talk to you. I–"

The man's bony hand snaked out and clamped on the girl's shoulder so savagely she winced.

"I have nothing to talk to you about. You are no son of mine!"

With that he jerked Lolita around and pulled her into the hut.

Pedro stared, motionless, as though he could scarcely believe what he had just seen.

"He–he not let Lolita even talk to me." He spoke to Ron in his broken English. His thin young voice broke.

Awkwardly Ron put his arm about the young Indian's shoulders.

"God can change that, Pedro," he reminded him. "He can soften his heart."

Pedro still did not move.

"My mother, she not even come out to see me." He sounded as though the life had suddenly gone out of him.

"Your father probably wouldn't let her."

Gently Ron turned Pedro about and guided him back along the path in the direction they had come. It was several minutes before he spoke again.

"Don't you think we ought to go back to the Aldrich's now?" he asked.

The boy was slow in answering.

"My mother," he repeated, "she not even come out to see me."

Ron did not reply. What could he say to the youthful Christian? How could he find words to comfort him?

"Now they never take Jesus as their Savior," Pedro said.

By this time they had left the village and were on the path that led down the steep hill. Ron stopped and turned to his companion.

"Pedro," he asked, "did you take Jesus as your Savior the first time you heard the gospel?"

The Indian boy shook his head.

"What did you tell Rev. Aldrich?"

"Pedro get mad – tell him to leave me alone. Pedro spit at him."

"You're a Christian now, aren't you?" Ron asked quietly.

"Sí." Questions stood in his somber eyes. "Sí, I am Christian now, but–" His voice trailed off.

"You were angry because of the gospel," Ron told him. "Your father is angry because of the gospel. You are a Christian now, Pedro." He paused significantly. "Do you think God is so weak He cannot save your father?"

"No." Pedro turned the matter over in his mind. "No, God can save him."

"I think it is because God is talking to your father's heart that he got so mad. Maybe he is fighting against giving his heart to Jesus."

Before Ron had opportunity to say more, there was a rustle in the grass that lined the path and a small dark head appeared.

"Pedro!" the boy cried.

"Jose!"

Fright flamed high in the eyes of the witch doctor's son, and a hand flew to his mouth in warning.

"Sh!"

"What are you doing here?"

"I have to see you," Jose said.

Ron eyed him quizzically.

The boys switched to their tribal language, talking frantically in guarded tones. At last Pedro looked up at Ron.

"He say his father, he very angry at me for following Jesus," he repeated. "He answer questions for my father about future."

Ron nodded. He knew that most primitive tribes

were greatly concerned about what was going to happen in the days and months and years to come. Most of them had their oracles to supply them with information which they hoped was good.

"My father, he talked to the beans and the three crosses," Jose explained. Skepticism colored his voice as he spoke now in Spanish.

Ron could see that Jose didn't put much trust in his father's ability to tell what was going to happen.

"He talked to the beans and said, 'Anybody who talks to Pedro when he comes back–anybody who gives him to eat or drink or sleep, the evil spirits will bring bad sickness to them. Very bad.'"

Ron spoke up. "What does that mean?"

Jose hesitated. A strange look gleamed in his eyes and he glanced uneasily over his shoulder as though he was suddenly afraid that he had been followed and was being overheard.

"He said something terrible will happen to you, Pedro," he continued, "if you do not come back to the ways of our people."

A strange look came to the Indian Christian's eyes. "But why?" he asked. "I hurt no one. I only came back to tell our people of Jesus who died for their sin.

Jose laid a hand on Pedro's arm.

"You forget about this Jesus," he said earnestly. "Come back to the village and live the ways of our people!"

CHAPTER 7

THE WITCH DOCTOR'S THREAT

For the space of a minute or two, Pedro and Jose stared at one another.

"Come back to the village and live the old ways of our people, Pedro," Jose repeated. "You are my very good friend. I want nothing bad to happen to you."

Pedro was not swayed. Emphatically he shook his head.

"No, Jose." He was afraid and had to force out the words. "I cannot go back to the village and follow the ways and religion of our people. I'm a Christian now. I must follow the ways of Jesus."

Terror stood in Jose's dark eyes. His voice raised. "But you do not know how angry my father is! He says he will work bad magic on you, Pedro, if you not do as he says. He will do something terrible to you. Maybe he will even kill you!"

Pedro's face drained of color and a tremor came

to his thick lips. It was some time before he could speak, but when he did so he spoke as firmly as before.

"It makes no difference what your father or anyone else in the village tries to do to me. They will never take me from Jesus. I follow Him now."

Ron's admiration for the slight young Indian lad continued to grow. He put a hand on Pedro's shoulder reassuringly.

But Jose had not yet finished.

"This God of the white man is not for the Indian!" he cried, his temper flaring. "This God is not for you, Pedro. We worship the Indian God."

Ron Orlis started to speak but checked himself as Pedro continued.

"Jesus is not just the white man's God," the Indian boy said. "He also is God of the Indian. He is God of every man." Pedro spoke softly, but with great fervor. "The Bible tells that He came to earth to die on the cross and then came back alive again so you and I can go to Heaven when we die, Jose. He came to pay for our sin."

Incredulity flooded Jose's face.

"Why?"

"Because He loves us, Jose." Pedro took a long, deep breath. "That's why Pedro come back here, to tell you and the others about Jesus."

Interest kindled in the other boy's eyes.

"You say this Jesus died for Jose?" he repeated.

"He died for Jose. He died for Pedro – He died for your father even, who hates Him so much."

At the mention of the witch doctor there was a slight rustle in the leaves just off the path. Jose froze. His eyes widened. His lips parted wordlessly.

Ron grasped him by the arm.

"Jose!" he demanded. "What is it?"

"You come back to the village, Pedro!" Hysteria filled his voice. "You come back or there will be trouble! Much trouble!"

With that he whirled and went padding up the path and out of sight. Pedro and Ron stared after him.

"He's gone!" Despair was in Pedro's voice.

"He's gone." Ron expelled his breath slowly. "And I thought he was so interested in hearing the gospel."

"Jose scared," the Indian boy said firmly.

Ron Orlis's lips pursed.

"You know, Pedro, I hadn't thought of that until now, but you're right. He acted scared – awfully scared."

Ron turned the matter over in his mind.

Pedro, however, left his side and moved forward stealthily in the direction the sound of rustling leaves had come from moments before.

"See!" He pointed to the broken grass just off the trail that gave mute evidence that someone had been standing there. "Somebody listen!"

"Somebody was listening to us, all right." Ron straightened. "And I've got a good hunch who it was."

Pedro's eyes searched Ron's face.

"You think maybe it was somebody we know?" he asked.

"I think it was somebody who knows you."

The Indian boy nodded, almost imperceptibly.

"The witch doctor."

They turned and traced their way back to the mission house where they lived with the Aldrich family. It had been a long, tiring walk over to the village. The trip back seemed doubly long. Now and again, Pedro glanced at his companion, but he did not speak.

The missionaries were waiting eagerly for them when they got back to the house.

"Well," Gary Aldrich said, "how did it go?"

Ron dropped, exhausted, into a chair near the doorway.

"About like you thought it would," he said.

He told them all that had taken place. The missionary listened with understanding.

"I know that witch doctor, Ron," he said. "I'm afraid you're not through with him yet. He's an evil man, and if he thinks you might be working on his son, you're apt to have plenty of trouble with him."

Mrs. Aldrich came into the living room from the kitchen.

"My, but you look hot and tired, Ron," she said. "I'll bet you'd like to have a glass of ice tea or some orange juice."

"I certainly would."

Her husband straightened slowly in his chair.

"What do you plan on doing now, Ron?" he asked pointedly. "Will you go back to the village?"

"Oh, yes. We haven't even started working there yet. We didn't get acquainted with anyone."

"There are a good many places around here that would be easier to work in than Pedro's village."

Ron's answer was direct and unhesitating.

"That may be, but Pedro and I have made this a very special matter of prayer. We're convinced that God led us down here to deal with his own people, or at least to try. We have no other choice."

"I guess I knew what your answer would be, but I don't mind telling you, I am concerned."

Pedro came into the room just then and Ron changed the subject abruptly. Not until the young Indian lad was gone did he start talking about the village again.

"Would you advise us to move over there, Gary?" he asked.

The veteran missionary thought for a moment.

"If you didn't have Pedro with you, I'd say it would be sheer folly even to think about such a thing." He crossed the room and stood by the window. "It's true they are angry with him – so angry we had to get him out of the village for a time. But that doesn't change the fact that he is still one of their own. The very fact that Pedro is with you will make a difference with many of them." He expelled his breath slowly. "I think it might help you, Ron, although it is going to increase the danger. You're going to have to be very careful."

That night they had a long season of prayer.

* * *

Although Aldrich did not know of a hut located close enough to the village to serve Ron and Pedro's purpose, he got some Christian Indians together and built one for them, a simple mud hut with a grass-thatched roof. In two or three days it was finished and ready to live in. Ron and Pedro took their bedding, clothes, and food over to the hut the day after it was finished.

The missionary shook hands with them.

"I still hate to leave you two out here this way," he said.

Ron forced the thought away.

When everyone else was gone, he turned to Pedro. "It's about time we have our devotions and turn in for the night, isn't it?"

"Sí, señor."

Ron had just gotten out his Bible and was about to start reading when Jose moved silently out of the trees and stood in the doorway of the hut.

"Jose!" Ron cried in surprise. "What are you doing here?"

Pedro's eyes widened. He tried to speak, but momentarily he could not.

"Why do you come here like this?" Jose demanded in Spanish, his eyes searching Pedro's young face.

"We came so we could be closer to the village," Ron said, "so it will be easier for us to get acquainted with the people."

Jose's young lips were trembling with emotion.

"Look!" He tore off his shirt and turned to let Ron see his back. It was crisscrossed with livid welts. "My father, he beat me! And just for talking to you on the trail! What will he do to you if he catches you here?"

Pedro's face paled.

Jose looked around quickly, as though he expected to see his witch doctor father at any moment.

"You go back now, while there is time!"

He left as silently, as mysteriously, as he had come. When he was gone Ron turned to his young companion.

"What do you think, Pedro? Do you want to go back?"

Pedro spoke quickly.

"No, señor." Concern flickered in his eyes. "Unless you want to go back?"

"I want to stay." The young white man hoped he spoke calmly.

"I say to Pedro, 'God, He not bring you down here all this way from Mexico City just to cause trouble. He is going to bring your people to Jesus.'"

They knelt on the ground floor of the hut and prayed.

They went to bed early that night, but Ron found that sleep would not come. Every time he closed his eyes, he could see the wicked witch doctor leering at him.

He prayed again silently for the safety of his young friend and himself and for the success of their mission to the little Indian village.

He was still praying when he heard a faint sound outside. Breathlessly he opened his eyes and listened.

All was quiet.

Then he heard something else – the muffled thud of an object landing on the grass-thatched roof.

He looked up.

A crackling sound echoed through the still night air. Fear gripped Ron's heart.

And then he saw yellow fingers licking along the roof! *Fire! FIRE!*

CHAPTER 8

JOSE GIVES IN

For the space of a heartbeat, Ron Orlis stared numbly up at the crackling flames that were spreading along the roof.

"Pedro!" His voice rang out in the still night air. "Pedro! Fire!"

The Indian lad sat up in bed, the eerie yellow light of the flames revealing the terror that was etched on his dark face.

"Quick, Pedro! We've got to get out of here!"

Ron was already up, throwing their gear out the narrow door.

"Sí, señor!"

Fortunately, the grass roof was still partially green and did not burn too rapidly. That gave them time enough to get the last of their supplies outside before the rafters caved in.

"It was good thing you see fire, señor," Pedro said.

"We could have been burned alive in there."
Ron shuddered.

Pedro was right. They could have been burned alive in the hut. In fact, that might have been exactly what the one who set the hut aflame had planned.

A nameless, aching dread swept over Ron, but he dared not give voice to it. He dared not even give it place in his mind.

"Jose try to warn us," Pedro said numbly, "but we not listen."

The youthful missionary forced a weak grin to his lips.

"We weren't hurt. That's the main thing."

"Jose's father, he do this thing. He say he stop us from coming into village."

Ron stared at the flames as they sprang skyward, driving away the darkness of the little clearing with their harsh, angry light. Somewhere in the shadows lurked an evil hearted shaman, watching to see what they did.

"What do we do now, señor?" the Indian boy wanted to know.

"Wait right here until morning. Then I'll stay here and guard our stuff while you go back for Mr. Aldrich."

"Sí."

They stood in silence, looking into the fire until it died away to smoldering embers.

The next morning, shortly before dawn, Pedro trotted off in the direction of the mission station.

Several hours later he was back with Gary Aldrich and two Christian Indians.

The veteran missionary surveyed the burned hut quietly. "What are you going to do now?"

"That's what I wanted to ask you."

They sat down on one of the army cots. "Should we stay on and try to get into the village, or should we give it up?"

The missionary did not answer immediately.

"I think the witch doctor was trying to scare you into leaving," he said at last, "but I'd hesitate to tell you and Pedro what to do."

The missionary's mouth tightened.

"If you let him scare you out now, Ron," he replied, "you're finished as far as reaching anyone in the village is concerned. The old shaman will get more and more bold and make a real effort to run you out of the entire area."

Ron took a deep breath.

"And what if we stay?" he asked.

"That's the part I don't like to think about. He might back down completely at the first show of courage." The older man paused briefly. "And he might get so desperate that he'd try anything in order to get rid of you. In short, we can only guess what he would do."

Ron's eyes flashed. "If you'll help us rebuild," he said, "we'll stay."

They started rebuilding the roof that afternoon, but only got part of it finished. Ron and Pedro elected to stay out at the hut that night, even though the roof was not completed. Gary Aldrich stayed with them.

They took turns sitting by the fire just outside the hut but saw or heard nothing. If the village shaman sneaked down to spy on them, he stole away just as quietly without revealing his presence.

The following day they finished work on the roof. Gary Aldrich stayed at the hut with Ron and Pedro for several nights, but there was no sign of the witch doctor. The clearing could not have been more quiet had it been on Little McCoy Island in Angle Bay or somewhere on Harrison Creek. Ron Orlis began to relax a little.

"What do you think, Gary?" he asked. "Has he given up?"

The missionary shook his head. "That's hard to say yet.

That afternoon Gary Aldrich prepared to leave.

"What do you think we ought to do about making contact with the Indians of the village again?" Ron asked. "Do you think we ought to go back up there?"

Mr. Aldrich thought for a moment.

"I'm not sure that would be wise, at least for a time." He picked up a pebble and fingered it absent-mindedly. "To stay out here and show the witch doctor he can't drive you away is one thing. To go back into his village and defy him is something else. It could cause big trouble." He threw the pebble away. "If I were doing it, I believe I'd go over to the archaeological ruins and distribute tracts to the American tourists who come down to look at them."

Ron eyed him curiously.

"But how could that help to reach the people of Pedro's village?" he asked.

The missionary's eyes twinkled.

"It so happens that a crew has started excavating in the area and a number of Indians from Pedro's village are working with them, or will be. You could make contact with them over there."

"Sounds like a good idea, but what about the witch doctor? Won't he be nosing around over there, too?"

"He can't be in the village and over there at the same time. My guess is that he's going to be watching the village so closely to keep you from coming in that he won't think of checking anywhere else."

Early the following morning Ron and Pedro stuffed their pockets full of tracts and went over to the ruins. The Indian lad was not too sure he approved.

"But my family, they are at village," he protested. "No see over here, señor."

"I know," Ron answered, "but Mr. Aldrich thought it best for us to go over here, for a while anyway."

The hurt flickered in Pedro's eyes. "God, He promise to save Pedro's mother and father," he said, "but it is so hard to wait."

"It is usually hard to wait, Pedro," Ron told him, "but we have to wait and trust that God will work."

"Sí." The boy's face brightened. "Sí. Pedro trust." There was a busload of Americans on tour at the ruins when Ron and his companion arrived. They went among them casually, speaking a word to those who seemed responsive, and distributing tracts. A portly, overdressed woman scanned the tract hurriedly and turned on Ron.

"I don't know what you're doing down here, young man," she said officiously, "but you ought to be ashamed of yourself, bothering decent, self-respecting people with your propaganda."

"I'm sorry if I've bothered you." Ron spoke quietly. "That certainly was not my intention. But the Lord Jesus Christ means so much to me that I want to share Him with others. He is the answer to all my problems. He can be the answer to yours as well."

The look on her face changed slowly.

"What makes you think I have problems?" she asked.

"Don't you?"

She spoke woodenly, as though she could scarcely force out the words. "For the last year, life hasn't even seemed worth living."

The bus driver honked.

"Oh, my. I've got to run."

At that instant Pedro came hurrying up to Ron. "Señor Ron, Jose is over there working. He want to talk to us!"

Quickly Ron glanced at Pedro. "I'll be with you in just a minute, Pedro."

"But Señor Ron! Jose is here! He is working with the Americanos."

Ron turned back to the distraught woman. "Why don't you give me your address? I can have someone get in touch with you who may be able to help you."

While she scribbled her name and address on the paper, Ron sorted out copies of all the tracts he had with him, then handed them to her.

"I'll be praying for you."

Tears came to her eyes. "Thank you, young man. Thank you."

Pedro tugged at Ron's sleeve.

"Señor Ron!" His voice was guarded but taut with emotion. "Jose, he works with Americanos."

Ron Orlis's pulse quickened.

This was more than he had hoped for. More, almost than he had even dared to pray for.

"Are you sure?"

"Sí!" Pedro urged him toward the diggings. "Come!"

They went over to the place where two sun-bronzed Americans and half a dozen or more swarthy Indians were working. There was Jose, squatting in the sun. He was carefully digging the clay from around a small stone object.

The slight Indian lad looked up, recognition gleaming in his eyes. Recognition and a silent pleading for them to stay away from him.

"Jose!" Pedro called out under his breath. "Jose!"

Ron laid a hand in warning on his young friend's arm. "I don't think Jose wants anyone here to know that he's acquainted with us."

Pedro hesitated.

"But Señor Ron!" Hurt tinged the boy's voice. "We must talk to him again – about Jesus."

Gently Ron drew him to one side.

"We'll hang around here looking at things, Pedro," he said. "We can give him a chance to talk to us if he wants to."

They went over to the edge of the jungle to the place where the archaeologists had discovered a great head carved from lava. It was some twelve or fourteen feet high and half that distance across. The dirt had been painstakingly removed from around it, and it had been scrubbed to reveal the ugly flat nose and sneering mouth.

"Do you suppose this was once a god, Pedro?" Ron asked presently.

"No," a strange voice said. Ron looked up quickly to see one of the archaeologists. He was a tall fellow about Danny's age or a little older. "No, we do not think it was a god. We think it is a part of a statue of one of the leaders of the ancient people who used to live here."

Ron examined the carved face again.

"Now, if you want to see a god, take a look at this one we just found," the archaeologist continued, holding out a small figure of jade. It was a hideous thing, the head and shoulders were those of a man, with a duckbill hanging down on his chest.

Ron took it and examined it carefully.

"This is the most valuable find that's been made down here in twenty years," the scientist said. "Just thinking that men have bowed down to worship that thing gives me the creeps."

Ron and Pedro hung around the diggings until noon, trying to find things that were interesting so their loitering wouldn't be so obvious. As soon as the workers stopped for lunch, Jose sauntered toward them. When he saw that no one was watching, he motioned them in among the trees.

"What are you doing here?" he demanded in a taut whisper when they were out of sight of the others.

"We came over to give tracts about Jesus to the Americans who come here to look around," Ron said. "And to try to talk to anyone from your village who might be here helping with the digging."

"But your house, it burned down. You did not leave when that happened?" Amazed disbelief showed in his young face.

"We just put a new roof on the hut and moved back into it," Ron replied.

"But señor!" Admiration mingled with the fear in his eyes. "My father, he is very angry. He says he will make the evil spirits kill you if you do not go away after you get such warnings."

Their eyes met.

"We are still here," Ron said significantly. "We came to tell you of Jesus who died on the cross for your sin."

Jose pondered the words thoughtfully. At last he turned to Pedro.

"Will you tell me about it again?" he asked. "You tell me how this Jesus, He died to save me?"

Pedro swallowed hard and began to tell his best friend about sin and how it kept man from God.

"But the Lord Jesus, He came down on earth as a baby," he said. "He grew up like you and me, only He did not commit sin. No sin at all. And when He was a man, He died on the cross so we could be saved."

Conviction and remorse flamed in Jose's dark eyes.

"But how?" The Indian boy lashed out the words. "How can we be saved?"

"By confessing our sin and putting our trust in Jesus to save us."

With Ron's help Pedro found Bible verses to explain each step of salvation. When he finished, his friend's gaze met his.

"Is that how you are brave enough to fix the hut and stay there after my father burned it to make the warning that you should leave?" he asked.

"Sí."

The silence was long as Jose considered the bravery of these two.

"W-w-would Jesus give me the courage to stand up to my witch doctor father if–if I do l-like you do and f-follow Jesus, Pedro?"

"Sí. I guarantee it – if you put your whole trust in Him."

That settled the matter as far as the shaman's son was concerned.

"I will do it."

He spoke so quietly Ron was not sure he understood all that was involved. Hurriedly he questioned Jose about salvation and spoke at length on what Christ could mean to him.

Jose seemed all the more sure that he wanted to be saved. "Señor, I know what it means to be Christian. I see the way Pedro lives. I saw him brave as a mountain lion when facing my father. I want to be like Pedro."

The three of them bowed their heads and prayed in low tones. And not a moment too soon. They were just finishing when a shout went up from the foreman that the lunch hour was over and they were to start to work again.

Momentarily fear climbed into Jose's eyes.

"I will go now," he said. "You will not tell anybody what happened here, will you?"

Ron answered him. "Not until you tell us we can."

The Indian lad ran hurriedly to join the group of men and boys who were just starting to work once more.

Ron turned to Pedro. "Isn't that great? Your best friend is a Christian now."

"Sí." But disappointment flickered in his eyes. "Only that is not what I pray for most. None of my family come to Jesus yet."

Ron's smile was sympathetic. "I know how you feel, Pedro, but don't get discouraged. God chose to bring

Jose to Himself first. But that doesn't mean He isn't going to save your parents. We have to keep trusting and watching for the opportunity to talk to them."

The Indian boy nodded.

"I know," he said, "but it is so hard to wait."

Ron turned and walked toward the path that led to their hut. His young companion hurried to come up beside him.

"Pedro," Ron said after a time, "what is going to happen to Jose when his father finds out that he's a Christian?"

The young Indian gasped.

"I not think of that!" he cried. "It be bad! Much bad!" He grasped Ron by the arm. "We got to do something."

"What can we do?"

Pedro fell silent.

Ron broke a branch off a bush as they passed and fingered it thoughtfully.

"It is something for us to be concerned about, Pedro," he said. "That evil old witch doctor was angry enough when you accepted Christ as your Savior. And when you and I dared to come back into the village, he was so mad he burned our roof in warning. He's going to be twice as angry when he finds out what has happened to Jose."

Ron stopped suddenly. It was going to be bad for Jose, but it would be even worse for him and Pedro.

The old shaman would know exactly who was responsible.

Pedro turned to face Ron.

"What do you think he do to Jose?" he asked. "What you think he do to us?"

The young American strove to keep the concern from his voice.

"We want to remember that God is all-powerful, Pedro," he said. "He can protect Jose and you and me.

CHAPTER 9

UNEXPECTED DEVELOPMENT

It was almost dark when Ron and Pedro got back to the hut where they were living. They were both bone-tired. Still, they took time to have their devotions and pray for Jose before going to bed.

"I can hardly wait until we get back over there to see how Jose got along after he told his father he had accepted Christ as his Savior," Pedro said.

Ron sat on the edge of the bed and pulled off his boots.

"I wonder if it would be wise for us to go back over there right away. When we showed up today, Jose acted as though he didn't want to see us. It wasn't until he was able to slip away from the others that he came over to talk to us."

For a long while after going to bed Ron lay there looking up into the darkness. Jose would be getting in touch with them, he was sure. That is, he would get in touch with them if he could. His witch doctor father had beaten him terribly just for going down the trail to talk with them. What would he do when he found out that Jose had forsaken the ways of his people and had accepted Christ as his Savior?

Finally, Ron went to sleep, a prayer in his heart for the Indian lad.

Both Ron and Pedro thought Jose would find a way to get over to their hut sometime during the next two or three days. But, although they were close by all the while, he did not show up. Concern darkened Pedro's young face as he thought of his friend who had just accepted Christ as his Savior.

"I know it have happen, Señor Ron." He breathed deeply. "His father, he do something bad to him. Something very bad."

Ron tried to chase such thoughts from Pedro's mind.

"He might beat him and try to threaten him into giving up Christ," he said, "but he wouldn't actually do anything to seriously hurt Jose. I'm sure of that."

Pedro was unconvinced.

"I know him, Señor Ron. He bad man. He much bad man. He rather see Jose dead than to have him leave the ways of our people."

Ron picked up a piece of dry wood for their fire. "We shouldn't get so excited about this," he replied. "There's probably a very good reason why we haven't seen Jose. Maybe he's waiting to see us. And maybe he's working so hard he couldn't get over here to see us."

Pedro said nothing.

"Just you wait. We'll see Jose one of these days, and when we do, we'll see how foolish we were to be concerned about him. Everything will be all right."

The Indian lad walked to the edge of the little clearing and stared for a time in silence up the path toward the village. When he turned back to Ron, his dark eyes were pleading.

"Señor Ron," he said, "tomorrow we go and see what have happen to Jose?"

Ron took his time in answering.

"It might be a good idea, at that," he said presently. "I don't think we ought to go back to the village without Gary Aldrich. We might get into trouble ourselves and that wouldn't help anybody. But we can go over to the diggings where Jose was working when we talked with him the other day. If he isn't there, someone around there ought to know where he is."

Again that evening they spent a long while in prayer for the new believer.

Pedro was up long before dawn the next morning and by the time it was getting light, they had had breakfast and were on their way to the ruins where the archaeologists were excavating.

Ron Orlis started out at a normal rate of speed, but the farther they went the faster Pedro strode.

"Hey," Ron protested, "take it easy. You'll have us both worn out before we get there."

"Sí, Señor Ron. I slow down."

He did so for several minutes, then the pace began to quicken once more. At last they reached the old ruins and hurried across the clearing to the place where the crew of Indians were working.

Pedro grasped Ron Orlis by the arm.

"You see him?" he asked.

"He isn't on the job that I can see," Ron said, looking carefully about. "Maybe he decided not to come to work today."

The explanation did not satisfy Pedro. Fear gleamed in his eyes.

"No, Señor Ron. It not that. Maybe his father, he do something to him."

Ron had to admit that his own fear was growing.

He and his companion sauntered over to the place where the men were working. Dr. Sprunger, the archaeologist Ron had visited with a few days before, looked up and nodded, but did not speak.

"How's the work going?" Ron asked.

There was no answer.

He repeated the question.

Dr. Sprunger stopped what he was doing. "So-so."

"The last time we were here you had found a little jade idol that had you very excited. Have you come across anything else like that?"

"If we have, we aren't broadcasting it."

Ron stared at him quizzically, then turned and walked away. He and Pedro spent half an hour or more walking around the ruins and looking for someone they could talk to about Jose. There was a man or two from Pedro's village on the job, but the boy vetoed the idea of approaching them.

"They not tell us anything," he said.

Reluctantly Ron turned toward the road.

"I think we'd just as well go, Pedro. I don't think we're going to be able to find out anything here today."

They left the ruins and walked briskly in the direction of their hut several miles away. They had only covered a mile or a bit more when a jeep pulled up beside them suddenly and two police officers got out.

"You are Señor Ron Orlis?" one of them asked.

"That's right."

"You are both under arrest!"

Ron and Pedro stared incredulously at the officer, their eyes widening. It wasn't true. It couldn't be. This was just a bad dream and they would wake up before long.

But it was true.

The officer's voice rose impatiently.

"You are under arrest."

"But why?" Ron demanded. "What have we done that you are arresting us? What laws have we broken?"

"You'll find out soon enough."

"We haven't done anything. We've just been walking along the road minding our own business. You can't arrest us for that."

"Get in the jeep, please." The officer motioned imperiously toward the vehicle.

Ron still was not ready to go with him.

"I am an American citizen," he informed him. "And I have the rights of an American citizen. You can't arrest me this way without cause. I have a right to know why we are being arrested and where we are being taken."

The police officer did not change his expression.

"Get in the jeep, please."

Fear gleamed in Pedro's eyes.

"I know why this happen," Pedro whispered, leaning close to Ron. "It is the work of the shaman, Jose's father. He is the one who do this to us."

Ron saw that there was nothing to gain in protesting to the officer, so he got into the back seat of the jeep. As the driver started out, he leaned forward.

"Just where are you taking us?" he asked.

The driver backed around and drove off without saying a word. Several minutes later Ron leaned forward once more and tapped the senior officer on the shoulder.

"We'll be going near the house of a missionary friend," he said. "I'd like to stop and tell him what has happened and where we are so he and his wife won't be concerned about us."

The policeman half turned in the seat.

"He will find out where you are, señor."

Ron started to say more but checked himself. There was no use in talking to the police officer. He was paying absolutely no attention to him. He sat back in the seat and prayed in silence.

They drove down the narrow, dusty, twisting trail to the place where the road forked. Then, instead of going over to the Aldrich home a couple of miles away, they turned. Pedro leaned over to Ron and spoke in his ear.

"They take us to San Miguel. There is a jail there."

"How far from your village is that?"

The boy shrugged his shoulders.

"Ten mile, maybe. Or fifteen. Maybe more. Maybe less."

Ron realized that Pedro didn't have the slightest idea how far it was to the town where the police officers were taking them.

It wasn't long until they drove into the squalid little inland town and jerked to a halt before a ramshackle old adobe building that served San Miguel as a jail.

"You will please to get out?"

The officers were courteous enough, but they had a job to do and neither reason nor persuasion was going to keep them from it. An officer unlocked the jail door and, grasping Pedro by the arm, gave him a little shove inside. Ron was right behind. For a brief instant he and Pedro stared in disbelief at the slight figure in the jail.

"Jose!" Ron cried.

"Pedro! Señor Ron!"

Ominously the door clanged shut behind them. For the space of a heartbeat, they stared at one another, almost forgetting where they were.

"What are you doing here?" Ron's voice rose.

Jose stepped closer to him, excitement glittering like twin flames in his eyes – excitement mingled with fear.

"They say I am here for the same thing you are here for. They came to my house early this morning and brought me here."

"But why?" Ron insisted. "What do they say you've done?"

The words tumbled out of Jose in a torrent now that he had started to talk.

"Do you remember the little green god Señor Sprunger showed you the day I became a Christian?" he asked.

Ron nodded. "I don't think I'll ever forget it. It was one of the ugliest things I've ever seen in all my life."

"They say I helped you steal it," Jose continued. "They say I have to stay here until I tell them that you paid me to help you steal the idol."

Ron was stunned.

"But we didn't steal it. We didn't even see it again after we gave it back to Dr. Sprunger." The corners of his mouth tightened. "Why would they think we would steal such a thing?"

A strange light gleamed in Jose's eyes.

"My father, he made them think we are the thieves." His voice was taut with fear. "He followed you when you came to the place where I worked for the Americanos. He saw Señor Sprunger show you the little green god."

Slowly Ron went over and sat down on the rickety bench.

"But why would he do a thing like that to you – his own son?"

Jose's throat knotted and he swallowed hard.

"When I told him I am a Christian now, he was terribly angry. He said he would see that I went to jail – that we all went to jail if I did not come back to the way of my fathers."

Pedro broke in hurriedly.

"Sí. He do anything, Señor Ron."

Ron got to his feet and paced to the barred window, where he stood for a time, staring pensively out across the hot, dusty village. At last he turned to the boys who were with him.

"The question we've got to ask ourselves," he said, "is how are we going to get out of here?"

"It not be easy," Pedro observed.

"If we just had some way of getting word to the judge that we're being held without bail, I think we could get released," he said. "I'm sure your law provides for bail until the day of the trial."

Jose answered him hesitantly. "There is no judge in San Miguel."

Ron caught his breath sharply.

"No judge lives here," the Indian boy repeated. "He comes here every five or six weeks to hold court."

Ron's heart sank within him.

"You–you mean we might have to stay in jail that long?"

Pedro nodded.

"One time my father, he was in jail. They kept him there for two or three months before the judge had his trial and let him go."

Ron ran his fingers through his hair. He began to see what the old shaman had in mind. Ron and the boys weren't in jail overnight, or even for a day or two. He had planned it cleverly. He knew how to keep them there for weeks – perhaps even months – in the hope that Pedro and Jose would get so despondent they would renounce Christ and come back to the village as pagans again.

"Do you fellows know anyone who lives here in town?" he asked. "Anyone we could trust to take a message to Gary Aldrich?"

Simultaneously they shook their heads.

"No, Señor Ron," Jose said. "We know no one here."

"We've got to get word to Gary Aldrich. He's our only hope of getting free."

Ron straightened and got stiffly to his feet. Pedro and Jose eyed him mutely. They were expecting him to come up with something, to work out a plan that would free the three of them.

Grimly he paced back to the window again and looked out. While he looked, a dirty, ragged little fellow of eleven or twelve came stumbling into view.

There was a chance – just a chance. Quietly he turned to the boys.

"Pedro," he said, "do you think you can get that boy to come over here?"

Pedro stepped close to the bars and spoke to the lad on the outside.

The boy's head snapped around and he stared fearfully in the direction of the jail.

Ron whispered to Pedro, who was doing the talking.

"Tell him we're not going to hurt him, that we just want to talk to him."

"Would you come here a minute?" Pedro asked.

For a brief, terrifying instant the lad stood erect, staring at him. Then he whirled and scampered away.

Ron stifled a cry of protest and disappointment.

CHAPTER 10

FRUITLESS SEARCH

Gary Aldrich had been out in visitation all day and was very tired, but thoughts of Ron and Pedro were never far from his mind. As soon as he got home, he asked about them.

"Have you heard anything from the boys today?" he asked.

Mrs. Aldrich shook her head. "I've been expecting them all afternoon."

The missionary dropped wearily into a chair and kicked off his shoes.

"You don't suppose they tried to go into the village and distribute tracts and got into trouble, do you?" his wife asked.

"I don't think they'd do anything like that. Ron knows enough about that situation to stay out of it." His wife came over and sat down across from him.

"But what about the shaman?"

"That's something else again," Gary said. "Old Tulum isn't going to have anyone interfering with his standing as witch doctor without a fight. And, of course, if the gospel should take hold in his village, he'd be finished. He just might give the boys some trouble."

Mrs. Aldrich shivered.

"I can still see the look on that man's face when we took Pedro out of the village. I'm afraid he'd go to almost any extreme to protect his position."

"If they don't show up by tomorrow afternoon, I think I'll go over and see how they're getting along."

All of the next day the missionary couple waited for Ron and Pedro, but they did not make an appearance. The following morning Gary Aldrich took one of his Christian Indians and walked over to the hut where Ron and his young friend were living.

A vague uneasiness took hold of the missionary as he saw the lock on the door.

"There's no one here!" he exclaimed.

* * *

The jailer gave Ron and the boys nothing to eat the night of their arrest, but the next morning he brought them a little weak soup. All the time he was with them, Ron questioned him in Spanish.

"Is there a lawyer in San Miguel?" he asked.

The man's expression was blank.

"Would you tell him I'd like to talk to him?"

The jailer gestured that he did not understand. Ron swallowed hard and tried again.

"Would you take a message to the telegraph office for me? I'll pay you for it. I want to send a message to the American Consul in Mexico City." The man still acted as though he did not know what Ron was saying. In desperation the Orlis boy turned to Pedro. "Would you talk to him for me?" he asked.

"You speak good Spanish to him, Señor Ron," Pedro said. "He knows what you say. He does not want to understand."

Ron went to the bench and sat down, frustration and disgust written on his bronzed face. What could they do? He couldn't get word to anyone who could help them.

That afternoon Ron had a time of Bible study with Pedro and Jose, after which they prayed for freedom. Being kept in jail hadn't seemed to affect either boy yet. Ron prayed silently that it would not.

As the day wore to a close, the noises of the street in front of the old jail building began to cease. Still no one came near. Hunger began to gnaw at them.

Jose went to the window to look out. "I wonder if they're going to give us anything to eat today."

Ron shook his head.

The boy started to turn away but froze at the window. His eyes widened and his brown fingers trembled at the bars.

"No!" he exclaimed fearfully.

Pedro and Ron came up beside him.

"Tulum!" Pedro gasped.

The old shaman hobbled up to the jail and pressed his evil twisted face against the bars.

"You, Jose!" he growled ominously. "You like it here?" His son eyed him in silence. "You still want to follow the Jesus way? You still want to leave the ways of our fathers?"

Jose did not hesitate. "Sí."

Anger contorted the witch doctor's face.

"You come back to our village. You forget the Americano and his talk of this Jesus. You, my son! One day you will be witch doctor, too."

Jose shook his head. "No," he said firmly. "I have given myself to Jesus. He is the one I follow."

The shaman pleaded with him, but his efforts were useless. At last he fixed his attention on Ron Orlis.

"The evil spirits will have their revenge!" he grated darkly. "A thousand curses on you!"

The young Indian boys cringed.

"We do not fear the evil spirits," Ron said evenly. "The Lord Jesus Christ will take care of Jose and Pedro and me."

The witch doctor faced his son once more. "You are no son of mine!" He spat contemptuously. "Ten thousand curses upon you!"

Jose watched for a long minute until he was sure his father was gone. Then, still trembling, he went back to the bench and sat down. Ron put a hand on the Indian lad's shoulder.

"There is nothing to be afraid of," he said. "God will take care of us."

"Sí."

They were still talking when another sound came at the window. Jose put up his hand quickly.

"Sh! He's back!"

"We'll soon see." Ron raised his voice. "Who's there?" He spoke in Spanish.

The reply was in Indian, and the voice feminine. "Pedro!"

"Mama!"

"Oh, Pedro! What have you done?"

"We have done nothing wrong, Mama. I swear it!"

In the semidarkness Ron could see the Indian woman's features. She looked older than he had supposed. Her face was wrinkled and seamed, and arthritis had begun to twist her body. But when she spoke, her voice was that of a mother.

"Oh, Pedro," she said. "I am so worried about you."

He tried to act unconcerned. "It is nothing."

She pressed closer to the window and lowered her voice. "I followed Tulum over here after I heard the talk in the village. Pedro, you must give up this Jesus! You must come back to the ways of our people!"

"Mama, I cannot do that. I–I told you that before."

There was a short silence.

"You know what Tulum will do if you do not come back to our old ways!"

Pedro was a long while in answering.

"I know that the Lord Jesus will take care of me, Mama," he said. "He has saved me from sin. He will take care of me and keep me safe, even while I am here in jail. I am not afraid of what Jose's father may do!"

"But you do not know how evil he is. He will never stop until–" Her voice broke. "Even if he finds out I followed him here it will be bad for me, just for that."

"Mama," Pedro said seriously, "the Lord Jesus, He will save you from sin, too, if you ask Him to. You will not have to be afraid of Tulum, either."

Fear tightened her voice.

"Jose, you know your father! You know what he will do! Can't you talk to Pedro? Can't you make him understand how foolish it is for him to go against your father?"

The other Indian lad came up and stood beside his friend. When he spoke, confidence rang in his youthful voice. "But what Pedro says is true," he told her. "The Lord Jesus, He will take care of us. We do not have to worry about what my father may do."

* * *

Gary Aldrich stood at the door of the hut, tugging thoughtfully at the lobe of his ear. His Indian companion eyed him in silence.

"What do you think has happened?" the missionary asked him.

"There is no sign of trouble."

There was only one thing to do now. They had to go over to the village and find out what they could.

"Do you want to go with me to Tulum's village?" he asked his Indian friend.

There was no hesitation. "Sí."

It was only a little more than half an hour's walk from the hut to the village. Once in the Indian settlement the missionary stopped the first man he met.

"Have you seen Pedro and the young Americano?" Fear glinted in the Indian's eyes. "No, señor. They not be here." Then he quickly turned and hurried away.

Fifty yards or so farther down the path they met another Indian and Gary repeated his question.

"He come here one time only." He held up his index finger.

"Have you heard anything about them? Do you know where they are now?"

The Indian shook his head.

Gary Aldrich and his Christian companion walked slowly about the village, talking with Indians he knew – Indians he had helped with food or medicine or clothing in times past. Indians he thought might be able to give him some information. But no one professed to have seen or to know anything about Ron Orlis and Pedro.

As they continued their search without success his heart grew increasingly heavy. There was something terribly wrong!

At last Gary Aldrich turned to his Christian

Indian friend. Discouragement bent his shoulders slightly and tinged his voice.

"They act as though they know something, but they are all afraid to tell us," he said.

They had walked to the outer edge of the village when the Indian laid a hand on Gary's arm.

"Señor," he said softly, "someone is coming who would talk with you."

A gaunt, hollow-eyed woman was hobbling up a side path in a desperate attempt to catch up with them. Aldrich turned and waited for her. It was Pedro's mother!

"You are the friend of Pedro and his new Americano friend?" she asked fearfully.

"Yes," he said. "I am Pedro's friend." Excitement gripped him. "Do you know where he is?"

"Sí. He and his Americano friend and Jose are in San Miguel in jail!"

Gary Aldrich caught his breath.

"Sí!" Her eyes flashed. "And it is your fault! You came and taught Pedro the ways of this Jesus. You turned him away from the paths of our fathers! You are the one who caused all the trouble!"

CHAPTER 11

FRIEND IN NEED

For the moment the missionary ignored the Indian woman's outburst entirely.

"Why are they in jail?" he demanded. "What have they done?"

"They say they stole an idol from the Americanos who are working at the place of the ancient people," she replied.

"But they wouldn't steal anything from anyone. I'd stake my life on it. They're Christians!"

The Indian woman's voice raised hotly.

"That is what they say they did! My Pedro, he is in jail, and it is your fault, señor. You have turned my son away from me, even as you have turned him away from the ways of his father and his father's father."

Gary Aldrich spoke quietly to her.

"I haven't turned Pedro away from you. He is still your son. He loves you very much."

"It is only words you are speaking," she went on. "He left us, didn't he? He left our ways."

"He left your ways because he found the Way." Gary Aldrich paused for a moment or two. "Do you know why he came back here after going to Mexico City?" His eyes met hers and held there forcibly. "Pedro came back because he loved his family. He loved you so much he wanted to talk with you about the Lord Jesus Christ. He wanted to tell you what Jesus has done in his life. He wanted to win you to Christ so you could be in Heaven with him when you die."

A strange look came over her face.

"Tulum says you taught Pedro to hate us," she continued. "He cares nothing for his family anymore. He does not want to be with his mother and father."

"Tulum does not tell the truth when he speaks so," Aldrich replied.

"You do not lie to me?"

"I am telling you the truth, señora. Pedro came back to see you, even though he knew what Tulum might do to him. He knows that unless you repent of sin and put your trust in the Lord Jesus Christ to save you, you will not be in Heaven with him. He wanted that so much, he dared to come back just to try and talk to you."

The missionary could not be sure, but he thought he saw a tear glisten in the woman's eyes.

She laid a work-worn hand on his arm.

"Will you do something for my son?"

He smiled reassuringly.

"I will do all I can for your son, señora. And I will be praying for you, too."

She left the same way she had come, only more slowly. Gary Aldrich stared after her until she was out of sight. Then he and his Indian companion continued on their way.

They hurried back to the mission as quickly as possible. Gary got his pickup truck and drove to San Miguel. Without stopping at the jail, he went straight to the office of the chief of police, a squalid, dirty little building on the town's only street. The chief was friendly and courteous, but unrelenting.

"No, señor," he said. "I am sorry, but I can do nothing. The Americano has signed the complaint. My hands, they are tied. When the judge comes, your Americano friend and the Indian boys will be given a fair trial. You come and talk then."

Gary was as insistent as the chief of police was evasive. "When will the judge come?"

The chief shrugged. "Who knows? Maybe next week. Maybe the week after next. But he will come sometime."

The missionary pressed as hard as he could for the boys' release, but it was useless. At last he left and went over to the jail to talk with them.

"I'm going to see Dr. Sprunger the first thing in the morning," he said in Spanish. "I may be able to get him to withdraw the charges he filed."

Ron replied in English. "I don't mean that I won't be glad to get out of here, Gary," he said, "but honestly, this has been a tremendous experience. I've never gone through anything quite like it."

The missionary stared at him. "What do you mean by that?"

"You should have heard Pedro and Jose talk to their parents. Neither one has been a Christian very long, but they have greater faith and understanding than you'll find in a lot of people who have known the Lord for a long time."

By the time Gary got back home there wasn't time for him to go over to talk with the archaeologist that evening. However, he made the trip early the following morning.

"Did you find the jade image you claim the boys stole, Dr. Sprunger?" he asked. "Did they have it in their possession?"

"They knew better than to keep it around."

"What makes you think Ron and the Indian boys took it?" Aldrich persisted. "Surely there were a number of others who knew where it was."

"This Ron Orlis was the only one I showed it to who would have any idea of its value," the archaeologist went on. "Besides, we have an Indian who saw Orlis talking with Jose, one of the lads who worked for us. A little later he saw the Indian boy go over and slip it in his pocket."

"The fellow's name was Tulum, wasn't it?" Aldrich asked suddenly.

Dr. Sprunger straightened. "How did you know that?"

"I know the old rascal."

"He said he's the father of Jose." Sprunger sat down on a pile of dirt and moved a small clod with his foot. "He said that ever since the young American came around, his son has been everything a son should not be. To tell you the truth, I felt sorry for the fellow." He got to his feet. "And I don't mind telling you that I've only got contempt for a man like Orlis who would associate with Indian boys and induce them to steal for him."

"I'm afraid old Tulum has taken you in, Dr. Sprunger," the missionary said. "He's Jose's father, all right, but he's also the village witch doctor."

The archaeologist's eyes narrowed. "Are you telling me the truth?"

"That's exactly right. You can ask any of the Indians in your work crew. Tulum is the shaman. Right now he's furious with Ron Orlis because he led Jose to Christ. Tulum knows now that his son will not come back to the old ways, and he won't take over as witch doctor when Tulum is too old to do so. He knows, too, that if Christianity gets a strong hold in the village, his own power over the people would disappear."

Dr. Sprunger shook his head. "But to send his own son to jail on perjured testimony. It just doesn't seem possible."

"But it is. You see, Tulum hates Christ more than he loves his son."

Starting at the beginning Gary Aldrich told the archaeologist everything that had taken place. He told him how he had led Pedro to Christ and how the witch doctor had threatened the boy so much he had to get him out of the village. He told him how the boy had come back from Mexico City to talk to his parents about Christ. How Ron Orlis, who had come down to Mexico to distribute tracts and sell books and Bibles, had gotten permission to leave the group and come down to this area with Pedro. He related how Jose had accepted Christ as his Savior.

"So now old Tulum strikes at Ron and the two Indian boys by getting them accused of stealing your jade image and getting them thrown into jail," he concluded.

Dr. Sprunger rubbed the side of his nose with his forefinger thoughtfully.

"I can't say I understand all of it, but I've been around these people long enough to know they have some strange ways. What you say has the ring of truth in it."

"It is the truth," the missionary said simply.

"And what do you want me to do?"

"I'd like to have you go with me to the jail to get Ron and the boys released. I'll personally vouch for their honesty, and if they are brought to trial, I'll guarantee that they will be there."

Dr. Sprunger's frown deepened. "What you say makes sense, and I'm inclined to believe it," he said, "but if the image is found in their possession, I'll have no recourse other than to take action."

"Agreed."

"And I'll expect you to produce all three of them for trial."

"I give my word."

Dr. Sprunger went to San Miguel with the missionary to talk to the chief of police, but he was as firm and unrelenting as ever.

"But I cannot release them," he protested. "They must go to trial."

"But I am the one who owned the jade image the boys are supposed to have stolen," the archaeologist protested. "I've changed my mind now. I don't believe they are guilty, and I want them released."

The chief shrugged elaborately.

"I am sorry, my friend," he said. "I am so sorry. But you know how it is." He shrugged again. "I only do what I am told. There is no way I can grant your request."

He went back to his desk and sat down once more, rummaging through a sheaf of papers as though he was very busy and wanted them to leave. Dr. Sprunger would have taken the chief's word as final, but not Gary Aldrich. The missionary moved up to the desk.

"Señor," he said quietly, "may I see the paper you have for holding Ron Orlis and the Indian boys?"

The officer looked up quickly. Color stained his cheeks. "Papers?"

"You know what I am talking about. Where is the complaint Dr. Sprunger signed authorizing you to arrest the boys?"

The archaeologist broke in quickly.

"I didn't sign any complaint," he said. "Tulum told me he would take care of everything."

"I thought so." Aldrich turned back to the police chief. "So you don't have a warrant to hold Ron and the boys," he said sternly.

The chief stood once more, blustering. "We don't need a paper to arrest thieves and keep them in jail."

"But who says they are thieves?" the missionary demanded. "How are you going to prove it?"

"Don't you worry about that. We will prove it when the judge comes."

His voice raised, but the missionary stood his ground.

"I think I should warn you, señor. Ron Orlis is an American."

"Sí." He spoke impatiently. "I know he is an Americano."

"If one of your people is put in jail in our country, your government wants to be sure he is being held legally," Aldrich continued. "They want to be sure the papers are in order. And if one of our people is put in jail in your country, our government is interested in knowing if everything is legal. And your country will be asking questions, too."

The officer's eyes narrowed. "You cannot scare me."

"You are the chief now, but will you still be the chief when your government and ours find that you hold an American in jail without papers?" Gary's voice lowered. "They may even put you in jail yourself."

The chief flinched. He sat down again and picked up the papers on his desk.

"As a favor to you I let the Americano go, but the two Indian boys, they stay in jail."

"But you have no papers to hold them either."

"The Indian boys stay."

"Is it because of Tulum that you are afraid to let Pedro and Jose go free?"

He snorted indignantly. "I am afraid of no man."

But the missionary knew better. He could read the fear in the officer's face. He could see, too, that further talk was useless.

CHAPTER 12

TULUM THWARTED

At first Ron was not willing to be released unless Pedro and Jose were let out at the same time.

"I know how you feel," Aldrich told him, "but we've got to be realistic about this. We can do more for the boys, and for you, if you are out to help than we can if you're locked up."

Ron's frown deepened. "I hadn't thought of it that way."

"You go, Señor Ron," Pedro said. "Then you can help us get out too."

Before Ron left, the three of them and Gary Aldrich knelt in prayer. Dr. Sprunger squirmed uncomfortably.

As they left the jail, the archaeologist turned to Ron.

"Just so we keep the record straight, Orlis," he said, "there's something I think you should know."

"Yes?"

"I think you're innocent or I would never have

come here with Aldrich to help you out. But if we should find that image in your possession or in the possession of the boys, I'll press charges on all of you, if it's the last thing I ever do."

Ron did not hesitate. "That's fair enough."

They took Dr. Sprunger back to the diggings and turned the pickup truck toward the missionary's home.

"I really appreciate the way you came over and got me released, Gary. We'd have been stuck in there for weeks."

"I'm glad you were able to be released, too, but we're going to have to find that idol and soon. Old Tulum is awfully clever. There's no knowing what he might do in order to lay this thing on you. Sprunger's on our side now, but if that image is found in your possession, I'm afraid we wouldn't be able to count on him."

They rode on for several miles in silence. At last Gary Aldrich spoke again. "You know, Ron, I've got an idea that just might straighten out this whole affair."

"What's that?"

"Are you game to go over to Tulum's village?"

"I suppose so."

They drove as far as they could and walked the rest of the distance to the little village where Pedro was born. No one spoke to them as they entered the settlement and walked deliberately down the path that served as a main street. However, somber eyes followed their every movement. At last they stopped a young man who appeared to be a bit bolder than the rest.

"Can you tell me where Tulum lives?" the missionary asked.

Momentarily, fright flickered in the man's eyes.

"Over there." He pointed to a hut that was somewhat larger than the rest.

"Are you sure you know what you're doing?" Ron asked.

"Don't stop," the missionary warned under his breath. "We can't let Tulum think we're afraid of him. He's been watching us ever since we entered the village."

As they drew near the witch doctor's hut, he came out to meet them – a squat, evil-faced old man with leathery skin and smoldering eyes. Surprise glinted in his face as he saw Ron, but he did not give voice to it.

"Greetings, Tulum. We have come to go through the hut the boy, Jose, lives in. We want to see the hut of your son."

Belligerence and pain mingled in the Indian's eyes.

"Son!" he exclaimed. "I have no son!"

"He is in jail in San Miguel and we want to go through the hut where he lived so we can prove that he did not steal the green image that belongs to Dr. Sprunger."

"You want to look in my hut for the stolen image?"

"We've got to prove that it isn't there. If anyone finds the image in Jose's hut or that of Pedro or his American friend, Ron Orlis, they will all have to stay in jail for a very long time."

A strange fire gleamed in the old shaman's eyes.

"You will not look in my hut!" he ordered. "Go! Go before I place ten thousands of curses upon you!"

Surprisingly, at least to Ron, Gary Aldrich turned and left without giving him any more argument.

"Now," Ron said curiously, "what was that all about?"

Gary laughed. "That is what is generally known as baiting the hook."

"What do we do now?" Ron wanted to know.

"We're going over to your hut and wait. I wouldn't be surprised if we had a visitor sometime late this afternoon."

They went into the grass and trees as they neared the hut and secreted themselves in dense undergrowth a short distance from the door. An hour passed, then two. The sun slipped down to the rim of the horizon. Shadows lengthened and began to deepen.

Ron leaned over and whispered, "It doesn't look as though old Tulum is going to fall for our bait, does it?"

The missionary started to reply but checked himself and put a finger to his lips in warning. Ron crouched tensely and leaned forward.

Somebody was coming!

Quietly Ron parted the thick grass and brush and peered out. Someone was at the door of the hut, all right, but it was not Tulum!

Ron caught his breath. A sharp pain knifed through his chest. It was not Tulum out there; it was Pedro's mother! She clutched something tightly in her hand!

"It can't be!" Ron exclaimed under his breath. "She can't be the one who stole that jade image!"

Indecision seemed to grip the frightened woman at the door of the hut. She paused, looking over her shoulder, as though fearful that someone had followed her. Then, with obvious reluctance, she forced herself to turn the lock. They heard a metallic click and an instant later the door swung open.

"Did you see that, Gary?" Ron demanded. "She has a key to our place."

The missionary nodded. "Do you still have yours?"

"I certainly do. I locked the door the other morning before we left."

"There were two keys to the lock. What did you do with the other one, give it to Pedro?"

"Why would he need a key? We were always together. The other key was kicking around the place somewhere."

Then they saw the Indian woman's head turn as her gaze was drawn irresistibly to a small clump of brush on the opposite side of the hut. Something in the brush moved.

"Gary!" Ron grabbed his friend by the arm and squeezed savagely. "There's Tulum hiding over there watching her!"

"That explains everything!"

The sight of the witch doctor watching her gave legs to the woman's fear. Quickly she darted inside the hut.

Gary Aldrich and Ron dashed inside after her. As they did so there was a scurrying in the brush across the way, but they paid little heed to it. The missionary grasped the Indian woman by the arm firmly, but without hurting her.

"So it was you!"

Terror-stricken eyes looked up at him. Her lips parted slightly, but no sound came out. Her arm was trembling under his grasp like that of a frightened rabbit. He released her.

"What are you doing here? Why did you break into our hut?" Aldrich demanded.

There was no answer.

Ron saw that she was fiercely clutching the green jade image. Shame and fear had stolen her tongue. She just stood there, staring helplessly at the two men.

"She doesn't understand Spanish well," the missionary observed. "I'll talk to her in Indian." He lowered his voice and smiled to show his friendliness. "We know you did not steal this idol yourself. We know you were putting it in this hut because someone else was forcing you."

She shrank away.

"We know you did not steal this," Aldrich repeated, "but the Americanos who own it do not know. They are going to think you stole it. They are going to bring you before the judge and maybe have you put in jail unless you tell us the truth."

Her gnarled hand flew to her mouth.

"No!"

"Tulum got you this thing, didn't he?"

The fear that flamed in her eyes at the mention of the shaman's name spoke more eloquently than a thousand words.

"Where did you get the key to this hut?" he asked.

Wordlessly she held out her hand and dropped the key into his outstretched palm. "You are not a thief," he continued. "I know that. But we cannot help you unless you trust us – unless you tell us the truth. Do you understand?"

She nodded. "Sí."

Gently the missionary continued his questioning. "It was Tulum who made you bring this idol here?"

"Sí."

"Why did you let him make you do it?" Aldrich asked, his voice showing his disgust. "You are not a thief. You do not steal."

Her lips trembled uncertainly.

"I did not want to do it." She had to force out the words, one by one. "But he said he would hurt Pedro bad if I did not do it. He said he would do something terrible to him unless I did as he said."

"And so he made you bring this image over to the hut where your son and the white man lived. Is that right?"

"Sí." She spoke haltingly. "He gave me the key." Her voice turned to pleading. "You will not put me in jail?"

The missionary's smile was warm and reassuring. "Of course we're not going to put you in jail."

Her eyes lighted with gratitude.

"We're going to need your help with something else, however. I'd like to have you go home with us and record your story of what happened."

"Sí."

On the way to the mission house that evening Pedro's mother was very serious. "You are not like some of the other white men who have come here," she said. "They did bad things to us. But you are kind. You are a friend."

He nodded. "Yes, we are your friends. But there is something else you must not forget. Christ is your friend, too. It is because of Him we have come here."

Questions stood in her eyes.

"We come to tell you of Jesus. We come to tell you how He died on the cross so you might be saved and live in Heaven with Him."

She took a deep breath. It was obvious she had never really thought about such things seriously before. When she spoke her voice was soft and filled with questions.

"My Pedro," she began, "he was a bad boy before he took this Jesus as his Savior. A very bad boy. He took things that did not belong to him. He said things that were not true. I worried for him. Then he became a Christian and everything changed."

Gently the missionary continued to probe in an effort to get her to think more seriously about what Christ could do in a life.

"In what way did Pedro change?" the missionary asked softly.

Her lips thinned and the muscles in her mouth tightened.

"No more did he say things that were not true. No more did he take things that did not belong to him."

"That is good. When Christ truly comes into a heart and a life, He changes it completely."

"Sí." Her words came slowly as she thought back over the change that had come into Pedro. "He worked in the garden, and he helped take care of his brother and sisters. And he told them they should be good and not do bad things."

"Did you know that is what he wants for you and the rest of the family?" Aldrich asked her. "He wants you all to have the same changes in your lives that he has had in his."

Her throat choked. It was several minutes before she could speak.

"And to think," she said when she could find words, "my son loved me so much he took the chance of getting hurt by the evil Tulum just so he could come back – and talk to me about Jesus."

Gary Aldrich pulled into the yard and stopped.

"Did Pedro ever get to tell you about God and His Son?"

She nodded.

"The Bible says, 'God so loved the world, that he gave his only begotten Son, that whosoever believeth in him should not perish, but have everlasting life.' That means God loved me – He loved you – so much

He sent His Son to die on the cross for us so we could be saved from our sin."

Pedro's mother was visibly touched. Her twisted fingers worked nervously in the hem of her shawl. When Gary Aldrich spoke to her again, his voice was just above a whisper.

"Wouldn't you like to accept Jesus Christ as your Savior now?"

"Sí." Her voice broke. "Sí, but I do not know how!"

"It is really a simple thing." Starting at the very beginning he explained that every person was a sinner and needed salvation. He quoted Bible verses that showed that Christ had come and lived on earth to save those who are lost.

Patiently he explained again and again how a person must confess his sin and put his trust in the Lord Jesus Christ to save him.

She hesitated. "But it is so hard for a person to be a Christian," she said lamely.

"It would be hard to be a Christian and live the way a Christian ought to live if we had to do it in our own strength," he went on. "If that was the way it had to be, none of us would be able to be Christian.

"But it isn't that way. God not only saves us but He promises to help us live the way we should if we put all our trust in Him. That is the wonderful part about it. We do not have to do it alone."

Her gaze met his. "Would God hear my prayers?

Would He help me to put aside the old ways and live as Pedro does?"

"God will help you. Of course He will. He helps every Christian who calls upon Him for help."

She nodded her understanding.

It wasn't long until Pedro's mother bowed her head and prayed for forgiveness.

CHAPTER 13

GLAD REUNION

Pedro's mother stayed at the missionary's home that night. She wanted to go along with them to San Miguel to see about getting her son and Jose out of jail, but the Aldriches thought it would be better if she waited until they brought him back. They did not tell her they didn't want her to go along because they were afraid the chief of police, in an effort to satisfy the old witch doctor, might try to put her in jail after losing the boys.

The two women went into the living room together.

"While they are gone," Mrs. Aldrich said, "I will read to you from the Bible and we will pray. Would you like that?"

"Sí!"

* * *

Gary Aldrich and Ron went back over to the place where the archaeologists were working. Dr. Sprunger came out to meet them.

"I didn't expect to see you so soon," he said.

"Perhaps not." Gary Aldrich's eyes gleamed. "But I think you will be glad to see us. We've got something for you."

The missionary held out the jade image.

"You found it!"

The archaeologist turned it one way and then the other, as though he still half doubted that it was actually in his hands again.

"I'll never be able to repay you for this." Then his smile faded, and his eyes grew hard. "Where did you find it?"

He was staring hard at Ron Orlis.

"It's a long story," Ron said, "but we got most of it on this recording."

They played the recording Pedro's mother had made. Dr. Sprunger listened in amazement.

"There's so much Indian in her Spanish I can hardly understand it," he said, "but I can get enough to know what happened. I would scarcely have believed it! Imagine a father doing something like that to his own son! I can't understand it!"

"It's like I told you the other day," the missionary explained. "You have to understand their hatred of the gospel of Christ in order to understand why they do these things. I actually believe Tulum would rather have Jose dead than to have him become a Christian – and he loves his son as much as we love ours.”

Dr. Sprunger weighed the idol in his hand.

“I’ll put this away where I know it won’t be stolen,” he said. “And then, I suppose we’d better get over to San Miguel and start things rolling so we can get those Indian boys released from jail.”

They drove directly to the office of the chief of police. As soon as he saw them he started to protest his inability to release the boys.

“I would like to let them go with you, but this thing I cannot do until the judge says it is all right.”

Dr. Sprunger was the spokesman.

“We got the idol back last night and what’s more, we found out who stole it. The boys are not guilty.”

The police officer eyed him suspiciously. “You have proof?”

“We have proof.”

The archaeologist turned to Ron. “Get the recording.”

They started it. The chief folded his hands and leaned forward as the recording unfolded the story. No one spoke until after it was completed.

The archaeologist reached over and stopped it.

“Well, there’s the story. Now what do you think of that?”

“Where is this woman?” the chief demanded, his voice rising in indignation. “We will arrest her.” He got to his feet and turned accusingly to Gary

Aldrich. "Why did you not bring her to San Miguel so we would not have to go after her?"

"You heard it," he said evenly. "The Indian woman is not guilty."

"She is the one who had the image."

"Yes, but Tulum forced her to take it to the hut in an effort to make you and the other authorities believe Ron Orlis and Pedro and Jose stole the image. Tulum is the guilty one."

"Tulum?" the officer flinched.

"If the woman is arrested and brought to court, that is what she will testify. And the judge will believe her."

There was a moment's hesitation.

"Enough of this foolishness," the chief said, sitting down and pulling a piece of paper from his desk. "Dr. Sprunger, write out a piece of paper that you have the jade image back and you know the boys did not steal it."

The archaeologist did as he was told. "I will decide later whether to bring charges against Tulum," he said.

As they went out to the pickup to drive over to the jail, Gary Aldrich turned to his companions.

"Don't think the chief of police here at San Miguel is typical of the police in Mexico," he said. "He's no more typical than a crooked officer in one of our big cities is typical of the police at home."

Ron smiled. "He's letting the boys go free. That's the main thing right now."

They drove up to the jail and Ron jumped out.

"Señor Ron," Pedro exclaimed, "we knew you would come!"

"Are you ready to leave here?"

They both nodded vigorously.

"Sí," Jose said, "but we have not been worried. We have prayed that God would help us get out – and He did."

The young Indians were about to crawl into the back of the pickup when Ron laid a hand on Pedro's shoulder.

"Mr. Aldrich has something to tell you."

The boy turned questioningly. "Sí?"

Gary Aldrich came over to where he was standing.

"I had a talk with your mother last night," the missionary said. "She accepted Christ as her Savior."

It took a moment or two for Pedro to fully grasp what the missionary had said. When he did, tears flooded his eyes.

"Thank you, God! Thank you, God!" He turned to Gary Aldrich. "Thank you, señor."

When they got back home Ron told him the rest of the story.

"And what is more," he concluded, "your mother said that your salvation made quite a stir in the village. Many people have been talking about it. Even your father said he would like to know more of what happened to you and why you are so different now."

A lump rose in Pedro's throat, and it was a minute or two before he could speak again.

"You think maybe my father will become a Christian, too?" he asked.

"It probably won't be right away, Pedro," Ron said. "You don't want to get discouraged if it isn't. Look how long it was before your mother accepted Christ as her Savior."

That evening after the boys and Pedro's mother had gone to bed, Ron sat in the kitchen with Gary Aldrich and his wife.

"What's going to happen to Jose and Pedro and the Indian woman now, Gary?" he asked. "Do you think it will be safe for them to go back to the village?"

"We were talking about that a little while ago," the missionary said, "and decided it would be best if they stayed here for a time. One of the Christians here will have room for them."

"I've been thinking about Tulum, too. What about him? Do you think he'll cause them trouble?"

The missionary's face was grim.

"Dr. Sprunger and I are going to visit Tulum in a day or so," he said. "I think when we get through with him, he'll be very glad to leave the boys alone. When he finds out we have the evidence to send him to jail, he's going to be very glad to make a deal with us.

Ron wanted to go with the missionary and Dr. Sprunger when they talked with the village shaman, but it was almost time for him to go back to the States and he wanted to spend all the time he could with Pedro and Jose. He taught them a number of Bible verses and went over some of the basic truths of the Scripture again and again.

When the two men came back from the village, Gary Aldrich was not so sure they had accomplished their mission.

"Tulum's a wily fellow," he said, "and his hatred of the gospel is as strong as ever. But we got a number of things settled. The two boys are going to stay here indefinitely, until we see that the situation has improved to the place where they can return to the settlement without being in danger."

"That's good," Ron replied, "but what about Pedro's mother?"

"I talked with his father," the missionary went on. "He wants her to come back. Before the village elders, he gave me his word that he would not punish her or attempt to get her to change her faith."

"The Lord has certainly answered our prayers," Ron said. "Of course I haven't been able to spend much time doing what I came here to do. I was planning on distributing tracts and selling books and Bibles. From that standpoint the trip has been a failure."

But the veteran missionary contradicted him.

"I wouldn't say your trip has been a failure. You came down here to witness so souls could be saved. You've been that witness, Ron. You've helped us a great deal right here at the mission." He took a deep breath. "And you set a series of events into motion in Pedro's village that resulted in the salvation of the boy's mother and Jose."

"Pedro's testimony won Jose," Ron said, "and you led his mother to Christ."

"We were all working together," the missionary reminded him. "The results are the important thing."

Almost before Ron realized it the time came for him to go back to Minnesota for his last year in Bible school. Pedro went to the bus with him and shook hands gravely.

"Thank you, Señor Ron," he said. "Because of you my mother is a Christian now."

"You thank the Lord, Pedro," Ron countered. "He is the One who saved her."

Ron got into the bus and found a seat at a window. As the bus started, he reminisced. What an adventure it had turned out to be! But it was worth it all when he recalled the radiant smile on Pedro's face as he had said, "Adiós!"

THE DANNY ORLIS SERIES

The Danny Orlis series, by Bernard Palmer, delivers a blend of adventure, mystery, and suspense through various settings—from the Canadian wilderness to Guatemalan jungles. Danny Orlis, an adept outdoorsman, skilled athlete, and committed Christian, employs his quick thinking, calm bravery, and biblical solutions to confront everyday problems and hair-raising dangers. Early stories focus on Danny navigating school life, sports, and outdoor challenges, while in later books, Danny and his wife Kay provide wisdom and guidance to youngsters facing lifelike situations and challenges. Having sold over two million copies, this series has made Palmer a renowned author in Christian youth literature. Palmer is also the author of the Felicia Cartright series and various other series for Christian youth.

AVAILABLE FROM WWW.ANEKOPRESS.COM

www.ingramcontent.com/pod-product-compliance
Lightning Source LLC
Chambersburg PA
CBHW060501300726
48975CB00008B/2594